DARK STAR PRODUCTIONS PRES
MOUN

MW00878782

Octavia Encore

The Third Novel of the mercenary Octavia Pomona

Michael Mounts

10/28/2015

Dedicated to my Mother, Shirley Mounts, because she loved me.

Octavia Encore

By
Michael Mounts

Part One

Field Exercises

Chapter One

At the same time we realized we had no supplies we also gained a critical piece of intelligence. We saw the trucks leave the base camp the army had set up, and Major Octavia intercepted a radio transmission from that same camp. The soldiers it seems had left behind a large amount of supplies back at their main base, and had sent a pair of trucks to fetch those supplies. A certain Colonel Heath had forgotten the victuals so critical to the Colonel's operational requirements. As we took turns listening in on Colonel Heath's radio traffic we had already learned the Colonel was incapable of going one night without all sorts of creature comforts, some you probably couldn't think of just off the top of your head. This presented an opportunity that we would be fools to not exploit. Our Major pulls out a map, and begins to brief us on her plan.

"They will have to take this stretch of road to return, they have no option about that, so we hit them half way down the path," Major Octavia says, pointing out the one lonely highway that is a choke point access to our current operational area.

"Deploy the soldier boys?" I ask.

"*Oh yes*, Commander Black, *two squads*," Major Octavia says with a hungry grin.

As we move out to set up our ambush my medic decides now is the time to show all her symptoms of those chronic conditions known as belly ache and butt hurt.

"We got a vacation last time, why didn't we get a break this time?" White asks.

"I've started to have my doubts about that," Tiger comments before I can tell White to shut-up. If you don't squash the cry baby stuff early it gets out of control, and of all people to get talky while we are in the bush and moving to establish an ambush, why is it Tiger who responds to the unauthorized jabber? Oh Tiger, she is my oh so dear sniper.

"What are you talking about?" Green asks Tiger, and I want to choke her. I mean we are on our way to set up an ambush, and these girls have decided to hold a union hall meeting about our benefits plan? Why is my Executive Officer breaking patrol discipline and talking like she is now?

"Well you and the Commander didn't really get the promised vacation. You had to help the Major. The Major took no time-off whatsoever. So there was no vacation," Tiger explains.

"You and White got lots of time off," Green says to Tiger, yet the statement provokes more superfluous talk from Tiger.

"My time off turned out to be some kind of blind date that helped our boss cement her corporate alliance with Irwin Grossman. Seiko *is just the kind of man I would want to meet*, but he's Irwin's cousin. Do you see how that helps the Widow? It's like I was targeted at a secondary objective," Tiger tells Green.

"The primary objective was?" asks Green, looking at Tiger like she's talking crazy.

"Irwin, because of what has happened with Irwin and *you-know-who*, our boss has had so much an easier time forming that strategic corporate alliance," Tiger says.

"What are you guys talking about?" White suddenly demands, raising her voice louder than I am comfortable with hearing. We are *on patrol en route* to set up an ambush.

"Also the Major took all those squirrels I bagged, and for what I don't know," Tiger goes on, her voice dropping in volume.

"Will the three of you try to act professional?" I hiss at them.

"I thought I heard someone mention my lovey-bunny," White says to me, sounding guilty and sad.

"Oh my God, you are doing it with Irwin," I say, because the realization has just hit me. I mean I knew it was possible, yet I never thought of it as real, not yet I hadn't. I mean we are talking about my little girl here, and she's found a man? I haven't found a man, and here she is having an affair with one of the richest men on any ten given planets?

What did she do to hook that guy? The last romance I got was some sailor *possibly* groping my goods while I was semi-conscious and *he* never gave me any flowers... or candy... not even a call the next day. If that makes me sound slutty then I will have to explain the extenuating circumstances to you later, just remind me. Now Tiger is talking again.

"No, it isn't so, Commander. Take it from me, and I never walked in on them dancing naked. Also I never saw Irwin doing some kind of bogie hustle while our girl twerked on his junk," Tiger tells me, her face seeming ironically *dead pan*? One thing is sure, I did not need that visual inside me head.

"Twerk on junk?" I say. It's the only response I'm capable of at the moment. I bet it makes me sound old.

No one says anything for a few moments. White is looking at Tiger like the woman has taken a poop on her breakfast. I have become beyond speechless, and Green also appears at a loss for words until she suddenly says: "Somehow my admonishment about pre-marital sex now seems moot."

"Not moot, just late," I say with a frown.

"I thought we were going to an ambush," White says, looking miserable.

"Why do you look so sad now?" I ask her, irritation surely written all over my face.

"Yeah, I mean because you're getting lots of loving, and on track to an engagement to a man who can provide you all the comforts and desires you could ever ask," Tiger says to White.

"Why are you guys talking like this?" White asks of the group.

"Oh come off it, since we left our old lives as frontier customs base officers you are the only one who has established a real and meaningful relationship outside the group," Tiger says to White, who is about to respond when Tiger goes on, cutting her off. "I mean we all saw how he acted when we came back from the Jasper Ignis affair. Irwin made a special trip just to see you, to see with his own eyes that you were unhurt and safe. Remember how he ignored everyone else and went straight to you?"

"I'm not engaged to anyone," White says.

"Just a formality is all that it seems, from what I'm hearing," Green comments.

"You guys think I'm leaving? You're mad at me because you think I'm leaving?" White says, and I can tell the course of the conversation has made her miserable.

"No one is mad at you. We are happy for you. If you and Irwin fall in love and get married then we wish you all the best, and didn't you and I already have this conversation?" I say, trying to reassure her.

"We need to get to our ambush," Green reminds us.

"The soldier boys are surely in place already, if the Major entered the strategy data correctly," Tiger reminds Green.

"They aren't supposed to operate without our supervision," Green says, reminding Tiger of important policy.

"That was in the old days, old rules, our old lives," Tiger says.

"We can't leave a dangerous military operation to be carried out by robotic automatons," Green reminds me.

"Hey, I taught the Major how to do the tasking program, so the chance for failure or accidental death is minimal," I say to her.

"There was another fun activity you got to indulge in while on *vacation*," says Tiger.

"That's why the soldier boys are not supposed to be without supervision, to avoid even the remote possibility of failure and accident," Green says, and she is practically pushing me to get back on the trail.

So we get to marching again, with me on point cradling my scout carbine. Green backs me up with the submachine gun she has brought. Then third in line is Tiger resting her sniper rifle over one shoulder. Last is White, toting her medical bags and with a snub-nose revolver on each hip. When did she start doing that? Is it something new? Is she just experimenting? Since when is my medic a two gun pistolero?

When we get to the ambush site the soldier boys are already perfectly in place. They are all crouched in the brush, long guns held at the ready, and each one has their visual sensor array trained on the road. I check, and see that they all have their auditory sensor array set to high gain. It isn't all technical specifications though, so when Green comes up next to me I listen close to her report.

"We're open-end box, not L-form, but it will work because we can pick up fugitives easier this way," Green tells me, so I know we are ready.

"We've got the diagnostic on the interrupter circuits up to date?" I ask, just to be sure.

"Yeah, I just looked, and we can be ninety nine percent sure none of our boys will shoot each other," she tells me.

"Acceptable percentages… by the way, where is the Major?"

"I guess she stayed back at our surveillance post?" Green supposes.

"We got to stay on our toes, she could pop up at any moment," I tell Green.

"Yeah, you never know where I'll be next," says the Major, at least it sounds like her voice, and when I turn to look over my shoulder, there she is, squatting in the brush just like the rest of us.

"How did you?" I mutter, and that's all I can manage.

"Just because I told you I've encountered operatives that are better at infiltration than me, do you think that means I'm incompetent? I could have taken the four of you out with a pair of throwing knives at any point along the trail you followed to this position," the Major says, and then she is quiet. Really, she drops that sort of thing on us, and then just leaves it there. She does it all the time these days, and I don't think its hostility or anything else but an uncomfortable truth. The woman is a cold… "Stop thinking awful things about me, Commander," the Major suddenly says, and would you believe I know her well enough by now that I can hear the laughter in her voice? Since she is speaking with spot on accuracy I must believe she's gotten to know me so very well, at least as well as I've come to know her. I hope my face isn't betraying too much surprise or embarrassment.

I look back at the Major and I see her wearing her black body stocking and a long black trench coat. I don't see a firearm in her hands, and she picks up on my curiosity.

"I've gone all less-than-lethal this time. I got my tactical baton, my monomolecular sword, and the Captain's gun," she says.

"What gun did Captain Malloy have?" Green asks.

"The one he pointed at his own head a while back? The silly goose, he was so upset that day. The black plastic thing, did you know it was only a stun gun? I don't think he knew, and I haven't asked him about it," the Major says.

I'm left thinking: 'the man who pilots our ship for us is suicidal, and the only thing we've done about it is take away the gun he *mistakenly* thought he could use to kill himself?' He still has access to nearly our entire armory. I mean he's the captain of the ship, what doesn't he have access to? That part doesn't even matter because he could just crash the whole thing into the ground.

"Why do we have a stun gun on the *Dowager's Daughter*?" Green asks.

"Because it's a lot safer to get trigger happy with a stun gun than any kind of hand cannon that could destroy someone, or more importantly something critical," the Major replies, that's the commanding officer I know and love, talking about human life as less important than physical assets. The Major, her posture stiffens, and she says: "It's in your hands, Commander."

I look around, and then I turn to Green and she's speaking to me.

"Network confirms two bogies coming down the road. Permission to go weapons hot?" Green says, and I give her a nod. I didn't tap into the network we have with the soldier boys, but I could have. As the Major left it in my hands, I have left the monitoring duties in the hands of my Executive Officer: Lieutenant Green. Both Green and I have the ability to monitor the soldier boys, those mechanical military masterworks. We can see what they can see, and we can hear what they can hear. It's a little more technical than that, yet you get the idea, right? I don't fully immerse myself in the experience while in the field, yet I could. As the 'command and control' module I could just sit back and direct things with the on the spot eye view my internal systems affords me, yet who wants to do that? Mechanical people don't necessarily want to live mechanical lives. I mean this is a two squad snatch and grab ambush type of operation, not a battalion or brigade scale assault. Put me in command of a regiment or multiple companies of combined arms and I will gladly plug my forward cortex into a master communications and control tactical computer. For bigger operations you will need to plug me in at every contact point I have and that means to either side of my head and the back of the neck. It's the same with Green. With the strategic analytical capabilities I am supposed to have I could possibly even direct global warfare, but who gets the pleasure of getting their hands dirty in a spot like that? I'm a hands-on girl, and you will see it, if you haven't already. God help me if they ever ask for anything more, like orbital combat?

Looking down the roadway I see the two trucks rumbling our direction, and with a pointing finger gesture of one hand, I authorize Lieutenant Green to execute our ambush. It's not like we haven't done this a hundred times before. At Green's command two of our soldier boys shoot out the front tires of the lead truck. There is no sound, just a flash of light and busted radials. The first truck comes to a hard, screeching halt. The second truck almost smashes into the lead vehicle, just almost. This is when another pair of soldier boys shoots out the rear tires of the second truck. The soldier boys begin to emerge from the brush, and I can see the soldiers who were in the cabs of either truck looking both surprised, and scared. Green leaves cover with *our* soldier boys, and every time we do this I'm tickled, watching her strut out before our enemies. She has a stare that could cow a death commando leading a suicide squad. Sincerely now, my girl Green has a way about her that turns most people's intestinal fortitude into runny jelly.

"Come out of there now girls, and present yourselves to your captors," calls out my girl Green to the soldiers in the trucks as she walks by the lead vehicle. She turns her head sidelong to look at them as if surrender is only a foregone conclusion.

We get four prisoners from the truck cabs, and to my surprise we get two more prisoners from the truck beds.

"What were you two about? Guarding the crates?" I ask them as I pass by, going to inspect their cargo.

"Don't tell her anything!" shouts one of our prisoners, and the raised voice brings me to a stop. I turn to look and see who shouted, and I see her. She has two bars on each lapel.

"I'll be with you soon enough, Captain, so for now just relax," I tell her and then I go to inspect the cargo in the truck beds. It feels like old times for a moment, because just this sort of thing was most of my career before prison, and then our rescue by the Major. Thank God I have spent more time with the

Major than I did in prison, and that should answer most of anyone's curiosity about why I am so loyal to her. I climb into one truck bed and open a box while my unit of four soldier girls stands guard over our six prisoners. I'm looking through a generous supply of tinned meats and mussels when the Major climbs into the truck bed. She takes a seat opposite me before she says anything.

"How interesting is it?" she asks.

"Probably not very interesting unless you are hungry, Major," I report in summary.

"I'm always hungry, Commander, yet you know by now that what I always crave is fresh meat, not any tin artifact," she says with a smile.

"It would be interesting to know if their Colonel paid for these supplies out of her own wages, or is she pilfering her command budget to cover the costs of her luxuriant living?" I ask.

"I need something tastier than that to sink my teeth into, Commander," Major Octavia tells me.

"Then you want me to destroy all of this as contraband?" I ask.

The Major looks at me as if I'm mad before she says: "Under no circumstances are you to dispose of these captured supplies. After all, we need to have something for evening chow."

The Major leaves me, and I continue to go through the boxes before me, with a smile on my face, because I'm seeing lots of good stuff and I know I'm going to get a taste of it all. I actually begin to sort out the stuff, bad from the good, and good from the best, when my attention is caught by a sound that I think must surely be someone getting a horrid smack across the face. I jump out of the truck and look for where everyone is, and nothing has changed except for the Major is now standing over the body of that mouthy Captain. It seems our ranking prisoner has fallen somehow.

Major Octavia looks at me, and she says: "This one will be interrogated first," as she points down at the captive officer.

The woman is face down in the dirt, eating road dust with our Major Octavia standing over her like an angry lioness on top of her prey, and I can only think if she still has any lip to offer, the Major will probably beat it out of her, along with her very life.

I head for the second truck, expecting to find more of the same as before: food stuffs. Instead I find cosmetics, a lot of cosmetics and I start to suspect that is all I'm going to find until I come upon a cache of documents. I take a look at the cover sheet, and I pretty much understand the term *'Tactical Strike and Elimination Forecasts'*. I still decide to open the cache and take a deep look all on my own. Whoever these people are that we have been sent all the way out here to surveil and investigate, they have more going on than poorly planned field exercises. I mean really, who sends six soldiers back to base for tins of meat and bottles of champagne? The logistics is asinine. Then again, we have less than they.

Taking the document cache in hand, I get out of the second truck to bring the papers to Major Octavia. By now the captive captain is on her feet again, but I can see bruises on either side of her face. She must have taken at least one more hit while I was in the second truck, and that just supports my suspicion this Captain is too cheeky for her own good. I hand the cache to Major Octavia while I'm still looking at the bruised face of our prisoner. Then I marvel at how easily the Major fingers through pages with gloved hands. Really, the Major's body glove tactical gear covers just everything, except her head... that must be why she always wears the dark glasses.

"You found this in a strong box?" the Major asks eventually.

"Nope, it was in the mix with all the other stuff," I say.

"You didn't have to break a lock to get at this?" asks the Major.

"No, just found it there," I reiterate.

"Commander, you have found here a critical intelligence estimate, or at least something that is supposed to appear that way," Major Octavia tells me.

"I only looked close enough to gain what I thought I needed before bringing it to you, Major," I say.

"Good then, because now we have so much more to talk about," says Major Octavia, turning her head to look at the Captain of the battered visage.

"Yeah, like why was an officer tasked with this supply run instead of just a sergeant?" I ask.

"Really, you think that's the most important question right now?" Major Octavia asks me with a grimace on her face.

I stand there silent for a moment, surely looking dumb until I say: "No, because the answer is readily obvious."

"Good, Commander," Major Octavia says, and then looking back at our captives, she tells everyone: "Right, figure out a way to get all that food back to our camp, along with these prisoners, and don't spare them any of the labor."

We leave nothing behind, except the trucks because we don't want to bother with spare tires or checking the vehicles for tracking devices. We perpetrate the cruelty of forcing the captives to carry the supplies in their boxes, even their officer is made to lend a hand. Hey, we have no plan to deny them food, so they are in part hauling their own rations. In fact things could get downright chummy, if not for that awful captain in the mix. That one won't shut up, and since Major Octavia is the only one who will deliver a smack in the mouth, the Captain gets to yap without cease on the march back. We have two of the soldier boys covering the Captain, and the prisoner can say whatever to them, or around them, they can take it and they won't do a thing about it. The Captain's loud mouth can go on being loud unless operational security requires something be done about it. What I mean is if the soldier boys think we are in danger of enemy contact then they will put a hand over the prisoner's mouth, or maybe a gun butt in the gut, whatever it takes. However we reach our camp without incident, and begin to settle in for hopefully a restful night. At least that is what I was thinking until the Major lets me know I have to assist her in the interrogation. I mean we were having fun, sitting around our camp, feeding our prisoners from the rations we captured from them. That Captain keeps mouthing off about how we can't eat their Colonel's food. That just eggs us on to keep foisting oysters upon our other captives, until we find the quail eggs. Those things are good, and most everyone partakes. The captive Captain is about to have a conniption when we open one of the bottles of Champaign and oh the fun we have serving it to the captive soldiers right in front of her. The teasing and torment goes on until Major Octavia decides to bring the Captain into our little command module.

Inside the little structure that we call a command module we have the Captain sit down at a tinny table and the Major takes a seat across from the prisoner. We are lucky to have this much space, I'm serious when I say the module is smaller than any extra-small mobile home, and that's before you consider the technical gear installed.

"So, everything I've seen so far is typical of Bellazar operational procedures," the Major says to open.

"I'm telling you nothing," the captive spits back at us.

Major Octavia gives an odd tilt of her head, and says to me: "Let the record show the subject displays full resistance."

I nod in response. If I'm supposed to be taking notes, I didn't know, because Major Octavia never told me to do any such thing.

"Did you know about this cache of documents?" the Major asks, indicating the papers she has sitting on the table before us.

The captive sits quietly with a mask of defiance for a face.

"Even a cursory look at these documents could be disturbing to certain people," Major Octavia says.

"You have no right to look at or touch anything you found in those trucks. You haven't even identified yourself!" the Captain suddenly blurts out.

"Well if you want something from me, you are going to have to give me something I want, value for value, and remember *you* are the prisoner," Major Octavia says.

"I'll tell you to go to hell," the Captain replies.

This is when the Major looks to me, and she says: "Handcuffs."

So I do it, we have a pair of cuffs in the module, and I put them on the Captain as the Major watches. I cuff the prisoner behind the back. The cuffs are on tight, at the narrowest of the wrist where it meets the hand. Also, I affix the cuffs to the prisoner's chair. Once I'm done a moment goes by before the Major speaks again.

"Now you see the price of being uncivil. There are privileges we extend to prisoners, and hands are one of the privileges," Major Octavia tells the captive.

"Do whatever you want, you can't break me," the captive responds.

The Major looks at me again, and she says: "Let the record show the subject was given every opportunity to be forthcoming, and unfortunately has refused."

"Yes, Major," I respond, while not exactly sure what is going on, other than I'm seeing the Major ask someone questions unlike I have ever seen her do before. Is this how the Major conducts a tutorial? Am I a student in her classroom? Then I watch the Major go to a drawer and fetch what turns out to be a snub nose revolver, and clippers.

The Major sets her tools down upon the table, and she looks at the captive in silence for a moment before saying: "These are the only tools I will use. You can make this end any time you choose, yet you must understand from this moment forward it is up to you to decide when then this interrogation will end."

"You can't torture me! You can't hurt me at all! There are rules about that, and anything you do to me would be a war crime," blurts out the prisoner.

"Bellazar is at war with Arcadia, and always has been, and yet I'm obviously not an Arcadian. While you may be a soldier of Bellazar, I'm not a real soldier. I'm a mercenary in private employ. What I do to you way out here, who is to say, who is to report it, and most of all, if you disappear, who will care?" asks Major Octavia.

"You have my whole detail out there. If you kill me then they will know something has happened. If you shoot me, or cut me they will see it," the prisoner says.

"Stop being so melodramatic, I'm interested in you telling me about this cache of documents that I already have possession of, so you can tell me or not. In the end it doesn't really matter," Major Octavia says.

"I already told you that I'm not saying anything. You are the worst interrogator ever. You haven't even tried to establish a rapport me. I don't know your name, and you haven't even asked mine," the captive Captain says.

"What do I need your name for?" asks Major Octavia as if she can't possibly see the relevance.

"I told you, to establish a rapport with your prisoner," says the captive.

"We are still talking about someone who will fit into several small shipping boxes when I am done with you, so it doesn't matter," the Major says as she begins to look through the cache of documents.

"Stop looking at those," the captive shouts as Major Octavia begins to thumb through the pages of the document cache and her eye occasionally lingers upon a passage here and there. Our prisoner tries to jump from the seat, yet I have the cuffs clipped to the chair causing the captive to be stopped short of doing what she intended or even standing to her full height. When the captive realizes the extent of her restraint the captive resumes her seat with some angry embarrassment.

"This is not going the way I thought it would," the Major eventually says after thumbing through a large number of uncountable pages, and then she pushes the cache of documents to the side.

"Can I help you, Major?" I ask, because I can't think of anything else to do or say and the moment and the silence is getting to me.

"I thought this was going to be bigger than it has turned out. I really did think I would be using these tools, and yet here we are with a captive Captain that is really just a messenger, delivery staff, a dogs-body. I'm feeling kind of sad now because there's no reason to torture anyone," says the Major. The moment would probably have more clarity save for the Major wearing her dark glasses. She always wears her dark glasses.

"You were never going to use either of those things on me," says our captive, sounding dismissive.

"Well not now, I mean not now that I know what your Colonel had you bringing to her. You didn't know anything about this stack of hard intelligence," says Major Octavia.

Our captive is now giving the Major an ugly frown.

"Oh, look at me getting old," Major Octavia says, momentarily hiding her face with her hands. "All I do these days is break bones and kill people outright. Did you know there was a time I really did cut people to pieces and just for fun?" she asks.

"Did you really?" I ask, because it seems like the Major has opened the floor to questions. For my daring I get a look I'm sure I didn't ever want. Not the first time it has happened, and I suppose it will not be the last. A few moments pass before the Major decides now is story time?

"I swear to you, I really have done interrogations that included the use of these tools. I mean that's how I was trained, so why wouldn't I use these things? Right now it's just that the circumstances don't merit getting messy," the Major says. A few moments pass before she picks up the clippers and goes on: "With these you have to be cautious of the bleeding. You can't confirm the intelligence gained from a subject dead of exsanguination." There is another pause, and then Major Octavia picks up the revolver. "The gun can cauterize wounds inflicted at point blank range, yet you can't count on that, not at all," she tells us as she appears to set the weapon down, yet she keeps her hand there, with the gun pointed at our prisoner.

All that being said, our prisoner is starting to look a little frightened, and I understand entirely.

Chapter Two

Yandi sits feeling very confused. He sits within an interstellar yacht as the vessel makes its way to a destination he is not yet aware.

"I can't believe you are the sole heir of Jasper Ignis," says the woman in white piloting the yacht through the sea of stars. She is dressed from head to toe in a kind of business suit, every garment of snow white silk.

"It was news to me as much to you. By the way, I'm still not sure about this course of vengeance you are talking about," says Yandi, shifting in his seat. He is a big man, so his nearly every move is audible, especially in a small area like this space craft. He is uncomfortable, yet it is mostly because of the level of suspicion he harbors for this woman in white.

"Are you going to let them get away with doing what they have done?" asks the woman in white. His doubts cause her to lurch forward in her seat, yet she strives to contain her emotions. It won't help her cause if she alienates the 'client' who now happens to be Yandi Yodel.

"I'm still trying to figure that out," Yandi says.

"There is no try, and you don't need to figure anything out. Yandi, we have been over this already, and we decided what we would do. Now don't go soft on me. Jasper Ignis was like a father to both of us, and we can't let interlopers encroach on family territory," says the woman in white.

"Excelentia, I worked for Jasper for over five years. You have been around for about a six-month period, standard time," Yandi replies, calling the woman in white by her first name. What were her parents thinking by calling her *'Excelentia'* is absolutely beyond the comprehension of Yandi Yodel, unless the woman adopted the moniker of her own volition.

"Are you saying you don't want my help? Because I can get off at the next stop. I can leave it all to you, managing the estate, dealing out retribution to the killers of your *father*, all of it, I can wash my hands of this and leave it all to you," Excelentia says, as she takes her hands away from the helm control of the interstellar yacht.

"No, don't do that, don't do any of it. Just stop with the crazy talk, would you?" blurts out Yandi Yodel, because he really has no idea what to do these days in his present situation. There is too much money and all of it is tied up in complicated accounts, none of it is *liquid*. There is all of the business holdings that belonged to Jasper Ignis and for some bizarre reason in his will Jasper left it all to his head of security, a man Jasper relied on less and less in the year before he died. The thing is Yandi does want vengeance, just not the way Excelentia talks about. Then Yandi is rubbing his elbow. The joint will never be right again. "I just need some time to slow all this down. I need some time to think," Yandi says.

"No, you need to act, because there have been too many insults unanswered. You need to strike back because there has been too much offense without reprisal. You need to take the fight to the enemy before they once again bring the fight to us," Excelentia says, speaking softly to Yandi. She is doing her best siren call, her best voice of seduction. Excelentia knows this is probably the fattest client she will ever have, fat in terms of funds, finance, and there is one thing Excelentia does not want, that is to leave money sitting on the table. In her line of work it can be feast or famine, and Excelentia is going to keep this fish on the line as long as she can. Indeed, she's going to spread the wealth around if she can, as long as it helps her keep the cash flowing.

"They did kill our boss," Yandi says, looking remorseful.

"It wasn't a killing, Yandi, it was a murder. They killed the boss, and they killed so many others. We couldn't even get a count of how many hands were lost when they destroyed our ship. The *'Busted Gut'* was lost so very fast, and we can be sure of only a very few things: that Octavia and her crew destroyed a simple ore processing industrial ship, and that very few members of the crew made it to the life boats," Excelentia tells Yandi, now reaching out to stroke the side of his face while she wears her best sad expression. *'Whatever works,'* she tells herself.

"So now we are going to see people who can help us find justice?" asks Yandi, showing so much less of the suspicion he had for her than he did before.

"Yandi, I'm taking us straight to the angels," she says, with faint smile growing on her face. Excelentia is feeling better at the moment because she is sure that she has Yandi in her clutches so much tighter now.

As Excelentia walks Yandi into the offices of *Xavier Gosling Private Investigations* he is mildly impressed with the job someone had done with the interior decorations. Lots of exquisite moldings everywhere you look, all of them painted white.

There was wallpaper of real fabric that was a very artistic recognition guide to small birds. "This is lovely," Yandi says.

"Try to keep it butch, will you?" Excelentia tells him with a frown.

"He's being complementary, Excelentia, let him speak his mind as he so desires," a man tells them.

Yandi and Excelentia look, and they see a tall man with thin hair, yet very dark. He wears an odd jacket, no one could be sure if it's a silk blazer or a smoking jacket, they are only sure his apparel is loud and gaudy. The man smiles, and nods his head to Yandi, then he extends a hand saying: "Yandi Yodel, please walk with me, while Excelentia goes to discuss your assignment with the rest of the help."

Excelentia is on the verge of screaming in outrage when she sees Yandi begin to walk off, joining the stranger who has invited him to walk just as someone takes her by the arm from behind. Excelentia turns to look and she sees a face she'd nearly forgotten.

"Let's ah, get your reacquainted, catch you up as it were, with all of your former colleagues, friends that is, you know, the girls you used to work with," says the man as he begins to gently redirect Excelentia in her path.

"Gomer Mosley?" exclaims Excelentia.

"Yes, well that still is, ah, that being said, that is the moniker that I employ, contiguous, so to speak," Gomer Mosley responds as he turns the woman around.

"You're not dead?" Excelentia asks, sounding as though she were full of disbelief.

"Been to the threshold, gone to the precipice, however you wish to express the notion, I have faced my share of peril," Gomer Mosley tells Excelentia as he begins to walk her back down the corridor, going toward a door she'd passed earlier in error.

"Wait, did I just see Xavier Gosling?" asks Excelentia, as she tries to look back down the corridor, only to be greeted by the sight of emptiness.

"Not so much, no, I can't say, can't confirm or deny, you know how that goes, lips sealed, not a word, we all have our part to play, and let's see about other things, shall we?" says Gomer Mosley as he stops at the door and opens it without any hesitation. Within Excelentia sees a room she's known well in the past, yet hasn't seen in so very long. She takes a good look before the firm hand, like a steel grip, that hand of Gomer Mosley directs her inside. This is another opulently appointed chamber, with the fine molding, the expensive and informative wall paper, and so many other things present. The space seems to be divided between luxuriant reception space and a modicum of office area. At least there is one desk and Gomer Mosley heads straight for it as soon as he has Excelentia inside, and the door closed... with the deadbolt locked.

"Excelentia Excalibur Excidium, so you have finally returned to the fold," says a woman, one of the four women present.

"No, not at all, and yet I see that Xavier still uses ultraviolence videos as part of his brainwashing," Excelentia quickly comments as she points to a screen on the wall that has been displaying the most horrid images.

"Oh, ah, that... well let's turn that off while we have our little meeting, this get together of ours, so to speak," Gomer Mosley says, and then he uses a hand held remote unit to turn off the video display. "You know, I say, you are fully cognizant, as well as knowledgeable that the mental acuity visual conditioning program is composed of many elements, that is to say diverse factors. Don't degrade yourself by declaring, that is to say, making the insinuation that our fine audio/visual training program is not of the best possible qualities, in its diverse nature," Gomer Mosley says when he does go on.

"Yes, violence, and sexual violence, so much in the way of diversity and divergent elements," Excelentia says in response as she watches the women in the room seem to come out of a spell once the video program has been switched off. "This exact place is what I am talking about when I tell people I escaped from a cult," she says at last.

"You were taken by a cult? Is that what happened to you?" asks Valeria Hogan, as she's still trying to shake off the effects of the mental conditioning device.

"We know her, right?" asks Nelly Silver, another woman in the room as she rubs her head to clear the fog as she points a finger at Excelentia.

"Did you say she was kidnapped by a cult?" asks Tanya Petite while she gives Excelentia a very odd look, as if Tanya were intoxicated.

"I said I escaped a cult," Excelentia reminds them.

"Well they must have been very sneaky if they got the bag on one of Xavier's Seraphim," Pricilla Hogan tells them in her forceful tone of voice, and her sister Valeria nods her head in agreement.

"Did you improve the mind control technology since I've been gone?" Excelentia asks Gomer.

"Well partially, the manufacturer has issued new versions periodically, with upgrades and patches. That is to say we've merely kept up with what's available to the market," Gomer Mosley replies.

"What are you talking about, Gomer?" asks Valeria Hogan.

"I so do not want to believe I was once under the spell of off the shelf retail mind control technology," Excelentia comments with a sour look on her face.

"I think this girl was once someone's mind-control slave," Nelly Silver says in a quiet tone of voice as she makes a small, and very slight pointing gesture with one finger.

"If it is any consolation, ah, well, if you would find it a comfort, you are the only one to ever break the hold," Gomer tells Excelentia.

"Oh, I understand now, she was taken by a mind control cult and since then she's the only one to have left the fold!" Tanya Petite says most excitedly. Excelentia can't discern at the moment if these girls are daft, or having fun at her expense.

"So now that I've brought Yandi Yodel here under my influence, Xavier Gosling is going to swoop in and snatch him away?" Excelentia goes ahead and asks of Gomer.

"Are we going to investigate a cult for our next assignment, or are we deprograming cult members, such as this Yandi Yodel?" asks Pricilla Hogan and her sister Valeria vigorously nods her head in agreement.

"Not to your exclusion. You brought us the fish on the hook, so only a greedy fool would cut you from the deal. That or a truly evil sort of monster, a real unscrupulous sort," Gomer Mosley explains.

"Whoever this cult of monsters is, Xavier's Seraphim will break their little operation wide open!" Valeria Hogan insists.

"He trusts me, and because I've come here for help, fully willing to cut you in on a share of the hefty take, I trust you will treat my mind and body as inviolate?" asks Excelentia.

"She has trust issues. It must be from her days in the cult. They violate you, mind and body. It's tragic, always tragic," says Nelly Silver. Gomer and Excelentia are working hard to disregard the others.

"You were the best operative Xavier Gosling ever had, and you think I would risk your return with some insipid hijinks that could undermine what appears to be a very lucrative proposition that you have dropped on my feet?" asks Gomer Mosley.

"She had an affair with Xavier? Does that mean she's seen him in the flesh?" asks Tanya Petite.

"At your feet, I believe the phrase is *at your feet*," says Excelentia.

"That sounds like Xavier, bringing a girl to her knees and making her beg him for it, at his very feet," says Pricilla Hogan, with a look of appalling lust all across her face.

Gomer Mosley spares the other women in the office a look of quizzical confusion, and then he makes to address Excelentia once again: "You have come home with a bucket full of rainwater in hand, so we would be fools to turn you away, or to mistreat you. The only question now is what does our new client want?"

Not far away in the enclosed arboretum maintained by Xavier Gosling, Yandi Yodel is excitedly saying: "Well if you aren't this Xavier character then at least tell me where I can find him. I mean I thought the whole point of coming here was for Excelentia to introduce me to the man."

"She can't introduce you to someone she's never met herself," says this oddly dressed man wearing his 'selling' smile.

"Then what is going on? I really want to know because I have been through far too much lately to be playing mystery games," says a stern Yandi.

"Relax Yandi, we only want to help you," the tacky suit man says.

"Well *who* are you?" demands Yandi.

"A direct representative of Xavier Gosling, here to negotiate with you on his behalf," the tacky suit man says.

"Negotiate what?" asks Yandi, coming to a stop in the path through the arboretum.

"We are contractors, all of us here. Excelentia Excalibur Excidium, Xavier Gosling, his Seraphim, all contractors and there is no one better to help you in your present circumstance," the tacky suit man says.

Yandi develops a look of disappointment and irritation. Then he begins to walk away even as he says: "You don't know anything except your sales pitch. You're a security contractor and private investigator. You can't help me with settling an estate, especially a massive one like that left behind by Jasper Ignis."

"We can help you, Yandi Yodel. We know things you aren't aware of yet," says the tacky suit man.

"What? What do you know that will hold my attention for even a minute?" demands Yandi coming to a stop on the walkway.

"Aborto Espontáneo Blanco. Also called the 'White Miscarriage'. It is a planet within a remote system discovered only in the last fifty years. Jasper Ignis owns that planet and in the wake of his death the scavengers and all the looters have moved in to pick clean the every resource. A planet that suffers enough already due to the circumstances of its development will be ruined by a ruthless predator you have already been forced to fight against. Can you tell me how well you know the name Morganti Bastille Giovanni?" asks the man in the tacky silk suit of so many gaudy colors.

From there Yandi Yodel speaks a great deal more with the tacky man, and all the others.

****

Things become boring after the Major got her hands on the document cache, the one I found, and gave to her. She reads every page, and then reads it again. This behavior is followed by a series of prolonged communications, all so deeply encrypted that I would wager not even the Major could tell you what was said even through Major Octavia composed the messages herself. Really now, I couldn't even recognize the alphabet she used, not a single character. I have to suppose one of the messages was a recall of the *Dowager's Daughter*, because the ship returns for us with haste. As the enormous vessel descends from out of the sky,

Major Octavia orders the prisoners freed. All save one.

"The demanding poochie, we are bringing her, after you tighten her shackles and lock a bag over her head," the Major orders.

"She's a source of tactical intelligence?" I ask.

"Yeah, something like that," the Major tells me.

Then all eyes return to the *Dowager's Daughter* as the vessel performs some kind of spin maneuver, probably to bleed off velocity as Captain Malloy works the station keeping thrusters to slow his vessel. The ship is going to hover overhead as we return on board, and it will be sad to leave all the wilderness behind, even for the comfort of indoor plumbing.

As we enter the ship Captain Malloy is there to greet us, and Major Octavia seems to be wearing her sweetest smile for our good Captain. Then I see her toss his stun gun back to him as she walks on by, only saying: "I borrowed it, thanks."

Then she is gone, and Captain Malloy is looking from the Major, to the one prisoner we have retained custody of, and then lastly to me. He asks: "Why have you brought a trussed up woman on board my ship?"

"She's a source of tactical intelligence?" I say, and too late realize I put no tone of authority into my words.

"Or something like that?" asks Captain Malloy, giving me his snide look.

"Hey, I just work here. So where are we going now?" I ask.

Captain Malloy immediately turns his head, casting his gaze toward a wall display panel. He begins to scroll through information and changes the display until he finds what he wants. "As I thought she is of course entering new data to the Navigation Computer, and without mentioning a word to me. I'd even guess she's doing this based on communiques that came to her from the Widow without you even knowing those messages had come," says Captain Malloy to me.

"I'm sure there is a big picture sort of thing going on right now that neither of us is privy to," I say with a little smile, trying to smooth things over.

"Right now your big picture is that prisoner you've brought on my boat, because not one member of my deck crew is going to spend a single moment dealing with the prisoner for you," Captain Malloy tells me, with a sharply pointed finger, and then he is gone. The Captain is surely headed for the bridge of the ship, or I at least would suppose so.

"Come on, we have to find a place to lock up *what's her name* there," I tell my people, pointing my own finger at the prisoner. This is when my people remind me about the small brig on board the *Dowager's Daughter*. When I ask Green about a watch schedule specifically for guarding the prisoner she responds with a skeptical look.

"We can have two soldier boys watching her around the clock, it will be no problem at all," Green eventually says.

"I want one of us to be checking in on her every four hours. The soldier boys are not equipped to spot signs of distress, and the like," I tell my people.

"I'll see to it that a watch bill is drawn up, Commander," Lieutenant Green responds.

"Carry on then," I tell them, and turn departing sharply. I go looking for the Major. I don't bother to secure my weapons in the armory. I don't say a word of hello to the deck crew, who I have missed while we did our recent and very odd deployment. I go looking for the Major in the very vain hopes that she may choose to tell me what's going on, or where we might be headed. Eventually I find the woman tinkering with what appears to be quite the oversized console. "Is this Navigational Central Core?" I ask.

"Is this you walking all about my ship with an unsecured weapon?" the Major asks, looking at my scout carbine with raised brows. Well it seems like her brows are raised, those dark glasses you know. When did she change her foot gear? We returned to the ship every one of us wearing tactical field boots, and now I see the Major wearing black platform stilettos as she kneels before the odd piece of computational gear.

"I'm just concerned. Major, I don't feel I'm fully briefed on our latest operational status," I say.

"Well on my ship *good girls* secure their weapons before asking their esteemed leader for the latest operational briefing," the Major tells me, and yes, she did sound both fully sarcastic and truly reproachful. Then we hear a disembodied voice.

"Oh come on and tell us while you know we are listening. Nothing is better than undivided attention," says the voice of Captain Malloy over the intercom.

"How could I have forgotten that he's always listening?" the Major asks me in a soft, quiet tone. Then she digs for a moment in her own load-out bag while I stand there like a dunce. When I next see the

Major's hand she has produced a device I hadn't seen in some time, yet I still recall her use of it. With the tap of a few buttons on the circular top of the thing it begins to expand. Green lights appear flashing in a subtle pattern, and then Major Octavia reaches up to set the device on top of the Navigational Computer. "We can talk now without anyone listening," the Major tells me, her eyes meeting mine for only a brief moment before she looks at the computer display again. This is when I lose my chance to learn anything. "What happened to the program I was entering?" the Major cries out of a sudden. She taps a few keys on the console, and when this produces no results she grabs her secret little *anti-monitoring* device. The Major tinkers with her little device for a few moments and then shuts it off. This is when we hear from Captain Malloy again.

"Octavia, what did you do?" the captain is shouting over the intercom.

Jumping to her feet, Major Octavia is shouting back. "You are speaking to your commanding officer!"

"I'm talking to the nitwit that just wiped all our pre-programed navigational data. I'm talking to the goof who will have to work late now helping me re-load our navigational system! Stay right there, Octavia. I'm coming down!" says Captain Malloy over the intercom, and then it goes dead.

I have no idea what to do at the moment, because to run away would make me look stupid, yet really all I want to do is run away because it looks like mommy and daddy are about to have an awful fight.

"He's coming down here. We'll be alone, working late, together. Here, just the two of us,"

Major Octavia says, and I see her tug at her bottom lip with a hooked finger. Is she checking her hair now? Then she looks at me to say: "I'm sure you have other things to do, like turning in your weapons? Really Commander Black, I expect you to be more professional. Now get out." That's the orders she gave me, and the last thing I saw as I left was the Major applying fresh lip-gloss.

So I go looking to see about my people, to make sure they are on top of things, what things I have no ability to say at the moment, and I suppose it shows.

"What did you see?" Lieutenant Green asks as soon as I walk into the berthing compartment assigned Tiger and White.

"Nothing, nothing at all, and why do you ask? By the way, our departure may be delayed. Something to do with data loss in the Navigational Computer," I tell them.

"We need to reload the Navigational Computer? Should I go try to help with that?" Green asks as the other Soldier Girls look at me in anticipation.

"No... no, no, no, I don't think that will help. That is to say I don't think the help is needed," I'm quick to say, and as always such an elegant speaker.

"It's just that I had to learn so much about that sort of thing during the *Stellar Mortis* affair. I'm sure I can contribute something," Green says, and begins to shuffle her feet as if she's to head off.

"No, I said no, I need your help here, or that is to say I need your help. I still have to stow my weapon, and log everything in, you know how that goes," I tell her. Then my dear Lieutenant Green follows me to the armory, looking at me the whole time as if I'm a world class nutter.

Left alone in the berthing, Tiger asks White her thoughts. "You think she saw the Major and Captain Malloy doing it?"

"Probably not, because we haven't been back on board long enough for them to get together, not in *that way*," White responds.

As I return my weapons to the armory and Lieutenant Green logs both weapons and ammunition as returned, she asks: "Do you know where we are bound for next?"

"I have no idea," I tell her, because it's the truth.

"Yet the Major knows?" Lieutenant Green asks.

"If anyone knows anything, then it is the Major," I reply.

"And she's not talking," Green laments.

"Whatever is going on, we will find out, for now we just do as we're told, yeah?" is what I say.

"The prisoner was secured, fed, and White did a quick medical check on her, just in case you wanted to know," Green explains.

"I did want to know. The unnecessary death of a prisoner is not something we want on our résumé," I say, affecting a smile.

This was the beginning of our trip back home, back to the Market Town, a place that is not really our home, yet it is the base of operations for the *Dowager's Daughter*, and if we do have a home these days, then it is this ship that carries us across the cosmos, safely shuttling us through the peril of the sea of stars. At least we thought we were going home. You can never return home, not without unexpected stops along the way.

What should have been five days of super-luminal travel through deep space came to a sudden stop at a point no one expected except for the possibility of Major Octavia and Captain Malloy. Well, they are the ranking officers around here. Me? I'm just a command module delegated to the service of Major Octavia along with my fellow soldier girls. Any questions you may have about pre-programed, and thus unwavering obedience should wait until the class breaks for coffee and other... *comforts*.

As I was saying we were traveling through space, from one star system to another, at a velocity of anywhere from fifty to five hundred times the speed of light, when of a sudden the ship slowed to a crawl. Please do not ask me to explain that, the physics are beyond me. While I try to say I understand the concept of a ship moving through the void at faster than light speeds, really I am only capable of accepting it as a fact of life. How does the *Dowager's Daughter* instantly leap across the void at distances of five hundred light years? I just don't know. I can only tell you that when we need to go someplace, then Captain Malloy takes us there, and no matter where you go, there you are. Now at our present moment we are as I said moving at a sudden crawl, and I rush up to the bridge to find out why. What I see when I arrive leaves me crying: "Why aren't you sounding the collision alarm?"

Major Octavia looks at me as if I have become ten times stupider than her previous most recent estimate. This doesn't change the fact that when I look outside I see a frightful vista of stuff that is all far too close.

Captain Malloy gives me a sympathetic frown, and he says: "We have good response from our maneuvering thrusters, so we won't be colliding with anything. Don't worry." Then he's returning his attention to the command console.

I turn my attention to take another look outside. I at least try to comprehend what I see with my eyes. What I saw before and see better now has alarms going off, if only inside my head. The *things* outside are monstrous huge, and are so much more imposing for the chaotic nature of the vista. "We stopped to look at the ugliest giant junkyard in all the universe?" I ask after taking time to make a most thoughtful evaluation. Again I have won looks of *'Who invited the dummy?'*

"Commander Black is your team ready to deploy for ship-to-ship combat operations?" the Major asks without giving me the courtesy of eye contact.

"We're fighting? I thought we were going home?" I ask, innocently, I swear. Still I win a look of reproval from the Major. For real, if she didn't have her dark glasses on to stop the death rays then I would be burned to a cinder a hundred times over.

"Commander Black, I am feeling generous, so I will give you twenty minutes and twenty minutes only to have your team ready to deploy for ship-to-ship boarding operations," Major Octavia tells me.

"Boarding operations, the load out for that?" I say, or I ask, what am I doing now?

"Nineteen minutes, Commander Black," the Major tells me, still with the death stare she has turned into a masterwork.

"Right, boarding load outs, toot sweet," I say as I flee the bridge to find my team and then try to figure out our gear.

Chapter Three

"Do you have the automatons ready?" Major Octavia asks the Captain of the *Dowager's Daughter* as they sit side by side on the command deck of the ship.

"You mean your prize crew? I think you need to tell *them* before this goes any further," Captain Malloy suggests, and he's glad they are alone.

"I've been busy, and it isn't their job to *know*, or to *question*, only to obey," Major Octavia responds.

"Theirs's only to do or die?" asks Captain Malloy.

"Hah?" is the puzzled if not incoherent response of Major Octavia.

"You do recall that Morganti had the obedience chips entirely excised, do you not?" Captain Malloy asks of Octavia.

"Worst move ever on her part, other than any time besides that when she failed to heed my every word of council," Octavia sharply replies.

"How much danger do you anticipate?" Captain Malloy asks.

"Isolated pockets, potential danger in remote locals, and I am pretty sure I can handle it with ease," Major Octavia responds.

"The group of you, or just you alone, because I don't want you taking unnecessary risks," Captain Malloy tells her, and then he's resting his hand on top of hers.

When Major Octavia feels something on her hand she turns her head to look. Even though she is wearing her tactical body glove she can still feel the pressure of his hand on top of hers. The moment has suddenly become strange. If this were an undercover mission and Captain Malloy was just one of the figures in her brief, then she would know instantly how to respond. Yet she isn't in disguise now. She isn't hiding who she really is behind a front of deception. Jack Malloy is part of her *network*, her ally, colleague, and *companion*. This is the man who has forgiven her sins, and given her his love. That was no small mountain for him to climb, yet Jack had it in him to make that trek. Jack Malloy is the man Octavia Pomona loves in spite of all his short comings, his flaws and outright failures. This isn't the man she settled for, this is the man her heart wants, and the heart wants what the heart wants. Such a tired cliché, yet every word is proven true. Why him? Why Jack Malloy? He's a stupid drunk, a pesky snoop, and there has been the appearance of other women drawing his attention.

Major Octavia snatches her hand away from under his and tells Captain Malloy the way things are in simple words. "I will do what the mission requires. Our desires are something to be set aside."

Then Octavia is climbing out of the co-pilot's couch to leave the bridge. She told her people to be ready for deployment in twenty, so she is far behind the schedule she has set.

I don't have to go far when I come upon Green. She's posted herself at a ship's passageway juncture that's both out of earshot of the bridge, and a good space from a ship's intercom. We can talk without too much worry about Captain Malloy listening in. "Ship to ship combat load out, she wants us ready in twenty," I tell my Lieutenant.

"You aren't sure what that would consist in terms of weapons and other gear?" Green asks.

"I know it looks bad that I admit it, but my every thought on the matter has been cloudy," I honestly admit.

"No, you suddenly have a lot to consider, and if the Major wanted us to be ready for this on a moment's notice she would have been drilling us for it, or at least given you parameters whereby you could have drilled us," Green tells me.

"Yeah, advanced word, it would be nice," I comment.

"Everything with her always has to be ultra-secret, yet there's nothing to be done about it," Green says.

"What we have to do right now is guess our way to a complete load-out oriented toward ship-to-ship combat," I tell my lieutenant.

"Then let's go, I got some ideas," Green tells me, and I let her lead the way. We round up Tiger and White, and then head for the ship's armory. Lieutenant Green begins to distribute weapons, provoking some surprised commentary on my part.

"When did we get these?" I ask, eyes wide as I look over the long gun I've been issued.

"The electro-pulse rifles have always been here," Green is quick to tell me.

"No, I'm sure this all was brought on board the last time *Dowager's Daughter* got one of her little overhauls," White says.

"They can't overhaul this thing, the corrosion is the only thing holding it together," Tiger says with a snicker.

I look at the woman, with all her fire red hair pulled back, in her olive tank top and tiger-strip camouflage pattern pants. She's examining the weapon she's been issued with a closer eye than any of the rest of us, yet she is my sniper, and for the sniper knowing her weapon system is her heart and soul. For any good soldier knowing their weapon is critical, yet it is especially so for the sniper. I find her comment about the extensive corrosion odd in how she voiced it. I'm used to Tiger being the most sarcastic member of the unit. I know Tiger will always be the most acerbic. Yet the tone of voice when she delivered her comment, it was playful, I even heard joy in her voice. "In a good mood?" I ask of her.

Tiger thinks about it for a moment, and then looks at me. "I suppose. Or perhaps I'm just not uptight about anything at the moment," she says, and then I think I heard a giggle.

I have no idea what Tiger would ever have reason to be uptight about. She's the kind of person everyone loves. Seriously, I've never seen anyone take a disliking to her. She's as pretty as a girl can be, and she dines out on that often, no question about it. Yet in the past she's always been our angry doubter, and sour naysayer. I shouldn't let her present good spirits occupy my thoughts; it's like looking a gift horse in the mouth. Not that Tiger has a problem with her teeth that I haven't mentioned.

"These weapons are good for ship-to-ship, yet we don't know if we are going to be Zero-G, or for that matter do we need to draw any kind of atmospheric gear?" Lieutenant Green asks.

"Don't ask me, I just work here," I say, and then remember I'm their Commander. Green, always in the darkest shades of olive drab combat fatigues, her perfect blond hair short, yet curled. When does she find time to do it? Green, my Executive Officer, I watch her cursory inspect the weapons as she issues them. She's the best professional I've ever seen. I almost want to say my soldier girls will be better off when she is in charge, yet that would indicate my difficulty with self-doubt is problematic. I can't be doing that.

"I need one of these?" asks White when Lieutenant Green hands her one of the electro-pulse rifles. This provokes a look from our good Lieutenant that I would not want to be on the receiving end. "I'm just saying," White responds in that little girl pleading voice she is want to use when under the eye of displeased authority. She sits there now in her white medic's fatigues and blond bob hair-do, examining the weapon as if it's an alien object. The thing is in her hands, yet the way she handles it is just as if it was on the other side of the room. Her behavior doesn't jive. I've seen her handle weapons before. Just recently she was sporting a two pistol setup that I had to wonder about. Then it hits me: my girl White is never asked to carry long guns. She's the unit medic so she's always burdened with her medical gear bag and what has always been her choice of side arm.

"No pistols for you this mission, just the Electro-Rifle and your med-kit," I tell White. She seems partially relived. Then Lieutenant Green issues a sigh of true exasperation. This has Tiger and White looking at her in expectation. "You two," I say to them, "make sure your weapons are ready to go, and see if you can find any light, compact respirators in here. Lieutenant, we'll have a word out in the corridor if you please." I lead my executive officer outside where I anticipate her venting the same concerns I am holding. I quickly try to cook up what needs to be said in this instance, and yet the need disappears when the Major suddenly appears.

"All right then, briefing time, where are the others?" the Major announces.

"In the armory gearing up," I report.

"Then let's head back in there and we'll conduct our briefing," the Major tells us.

So we walk back inside the ship's armory. I see the facial expressions of Tiger and White visibly register change when they realize the Major has followed us, and they stand frozen. Tiger is holding a helmet that looks like some kind of respiration gear, and White is sitting there in a posture that reads something between sulk, and lazy. When they see the Major, Tiger sets the helmet down, and White, she at least straightens her posture. I expected more, after all I have seen the Major say and do things that took the color from the girl's face and put the fear of God into her heart.

The Major takes a stance, something like *parade rest*, yet not so stiff, and she begins the *briefing*. "We are in close proximity to what is called by the Astro-Archeologists a *Void-Helkein*. That's what the Astro-Archeologists who first discovered the phenomenon chose to call it. Simply put the Void-Helkein is a massive hazard to navigation, and that's all it usually is considered to be, and yet others such as those archeologists and anthropologists, they consider it to be so much more. Yet theirs is a backward looking only viewpoint. A Void-Helkein is what happens over time when derelict ships collide, or at least come into the kind of proximity that leads to them affixing one to the other. Over time two or three derelicts in a cluster accrue becoming a hundred, if not a thousand ships fused together by the random elements of the void. True, most of the time drifting derelicts are smashed into pieces after being hammered into a useless state by the merciless forces of a chaotic solar system. Not so in this instance. What is outside the *Dowager's Daughter* right now is possibly a thousand old, abandoned warships that were, and still are considered broken to the point of being useless. Yet I must tell you that this conglomeration of ships from bygone days potentially has new value to those with forward thinking mindsets and there are experts out there this very moment verifying the potential value. Our Mistress readily agrees with the forward thinkers and their value assessment. As you may have surmised I have been in communication recently with Morganti Bastille Giovani, and among her orders was our visit to this very location. She wants it, the Void-Helkein, and we are here to help her achieve that very desire. The others here already on scene are hard at work performing the salvage, repair and conversion projects that will turn the hazardous mass derelict into a fully functional battle station. They have determined the isolated places that must see armed exploration before engineers and technicians begin to assess and exploit those areas for whatever value they might have to the overall project. This is where we find our role here. We will enter the Void-Helkein and clear out whatever may hamper this becoming a fully operational battle station."

This is when Tiger raises her hand, and I cringe. I never know if my Tiger is going to pop off with the worst kind of insolence. It is quite possible because of some strange synergy between Tiger and

Octavia that Tiger may instead be a perfectly respectful soldier-girl. When the Major gestures for Tiger to speak, this is what she asks: "What can we expect to encounter, Major?"

"That is just it, we don't know, and because of the factor of the unknown, those on scene had to call on us. The unknown danger is of such great potential only the best professionals can be counted on and called in for what must be done. We may find nothing, and we may come face to face with the most incomprehensible danger. Be ready for what you can't prepare for, set your minds in a state to come upon the unimaginable," the Major tells us.

"Was that a series of oxymoronic statements?" asks White. Again I cringe, and the sensation is accompanied by the desire to throttle my unit medic. Yet the Major gives the girl the closest thing she has to a beatific smile, that is to say Octavia is not staring daggers at the girl for what she asked.

"It probably was, and yet it is what must be said if I am to give you proper idea what you can expect. White, as our sole medic I will have you at rear position. If casualties occur, and that is always the possibility, we can't risk you being one of them," Major Octavia explains to the girl. Then silence settles before any more is said. When that does happen, it is the Major continuing her briefing: "We will divide into two teams. Tiger will tail after me as I investigate one suspect section, and Commander Black will be escorted by Lieutenant Green as they inspect another suspect area. As I have already mentioned: we have no idea how great or small the dangers are here, so be on guard, have your guns up, and come home to me in one piece."

That concludes the briefing and from there we are gearing up under the Major's direction, and that makes it all much more expedient as she actually knows what we will need and where to find it, as if she had set all the gear aside in advance. How do you anticipate any such needs? We are going to board an unknown and anomalous *thing*. Perhaps the Major has some small or even extensive experience with void operations including zero gravity combat? I'll have to ask her, *later*. Well actually after the *Busted Gut* incident we all know she's extremely deadly in a void battle.

Captain Malloy decides he wants to deploy by what he calls the *slide*. The thing is actually a super long tube anchored at two ends. One anchor point is the air lock of the *Dowager's Daughter* while the other anchor point is another air lock found on the *Void-Helkein*. Tiger and the Major are to go first, and I stand by watching them prepare for this unique deployment. They and all of us don harness along with our atmospheric gear. A cable has been run the length of the *slide*, and I'm told we will be affixed to the cable. The clip is a quick release rig that somehow *knows* when to detach, or at least is designed in such a way. The decision to deploy by such a technique is a huge surprise to me, and the biggest part of the surprise is that Major Octavia didn't argue or object at all when Captain Malloy brought it up. Did I even see a hint of a smile on her face just from listening to the sound of his voice? Never mind, now it is time to get our head in the game, and our mind on the mission, so I set to watching the Major and my Sniper perform the technique. They both disappear in a heartbeat and the only hitch seems to be when the Major does not report safe arrival, and then Tiger radios informing us that she has lost all sight of the Major. Strangely, Tiger says nothing about loss of contact.

This does not actually faze me because we know the Major always reserves to herself the right to do whatever she may please. The Major could be dead right now, having been gobbled up by whatever monster was waiting on the other end of the line, or she most likely went off on her own, confident she could leave Tiger all alone.

"She should have said something if she was going radio silent," White mutters, a sad frown writ upon her face.

"Rank has its privileges, and when you are at the bottom of the chain of command your privilege is silence," I say, probably because I don't like hearing her complain. No one wants to hear their children cry.

There is no time to think about it. Our brief leaves no room for staling or halting the mission because of *minor issues* like loss of contact with a team member. So we wait, Green and I, while Captain Malloy repositions the slide for our deployment. The Void-Helkein is big, massive, and there is quite some distance between the zone of the Major's deployment and mine. Yet Captain Malloy spends only a few minutes performing the chore. Were there zero-g operators outside aiding in the repositioning of the slide? Just one more thing for me to ask about later and I doubt I will remember. I still have to survive this ludicrous chore. So I attach the clip from my harness to the slide-line, and then give the Chief of the Boat a nod. He hits a large red power switch activating the magnetic tow system of the *'clip & slide'*. This sends me flying along through the slide down the line. I accelerate faster than I ever anticipated, and far faster than I thought possible. The Major did not tell us about this, and I have to fight my urge to scream. At the midpoint of the journey my velocity actually begins to diminish, yet for me it is imperceptible. I slow so gradually that when the automatic quick release clip does its job and I touch down inside the Void-Helkein I actually land softly. What I do perceive is that I fell to the floor, and that means somehow there is gravity at work inside the Helkein.

No time to dwell on it. Green is just behind me, and coming in hot. I move out of the way fast, deploying my electro-rifle as I move into the natural cover offered by the bulkheads. I huddle in a corner, the long bulkhead to my left and a one and a half meter aperture to my right. I look to see Green is alright, and watch her proficiency as she lands like a hunting spider, and deploy her weapon with beautiful grace. Well, beautiful grace as we reckon it. She's not a prima ballerina or anything like that you know.

"Lot of dust on this floor," Green says in the near absolute dark.

"Yeah, like a crypt. This should be a cake walk, easier than sleeping through a quiet night," I respond. Through the dark I can feel her stare. I just jinxed us, and only now do I realize it.

In that other, far removed part of the void-helkein, Major Octavia scampers along the overhead, crawling like roach, or a centipede. She swapped out a few regular pieces of her usual tactical gear, replacing them with the *wall walker* gloves and stockings that she now has on. Also the Major isn't wearing her special dark glasses. Not while she is wearing the atmospheric helmet required to navigate the Helkein. Octavia now wore other dark glasses that are made to fit inside the helmet, almost as if a part of the visor/faceplate. Octavia looks down the length of the passageway they've first entered, and when she sees movement, blue thermal signatures revealed by her special glasses, she calls out the shot. "Left, mid-level," the Major radios to her sniper over a secure radio channel on very low frequency known only by the two of them. Within the moment an electro-bolt lances the target.

It may have been sneaky or somehow underhanded for the Major and Tiger to establish their own private radio protocol for the mission, yet the two of them couldn't resist. It was needful, and they found it fun to occasionally share a secret however minor that none of the others had knowledge of.

Tiger continues to look through the special scope the Major surreptitiously gave her during the general issue of gear for the mission. It seems the Major wants to play a game, and Tiger is more than willing play along. "Two on the hard deck," the Major says over the radio, and Tiger makes two shots, the second shot just in time, because when the one loping critter saw its fellow fall after the arc bolt seared a cleft across its head, it began to move either for cover, or to turn in flight. There may have been some hesitation in the second target's movements, still Tiger made the shot, and down it went, a deep, dark burn cut across its flesh. Naturally the second creature died with more screaming than the first. The kill must not have been as clean.

After three shots of the electro-rifle the battery power cell is in need of recycle, a kind of recovery time and this is when the remaining critters in the dark decide to make their move. As if emerging from wood work, the monsters arise and start their run toward the shooter they know. Tiger watches the power gauge on her weapon fill out, yet not fast enough. She begins to reach for side arm, and this reminds she brought none.

Fixed to the overhead, Major Octavia initiates deployment of her own electro-rifle. She disengages the *wall walker* mechanism and begins to fall toward the floor. Octavia's fall leaves her spinning as she drops and shoots. Two creatures suffer head shots, and die instantly. Two others are hit by a single shot that cleanly severs a limb from each of them. Then Octavia hits the hard deck with a thud, and she is about to call out to Tiger to withdraw while Octavia covers her escape. Yet Tiger is shooting again, right over the Major's head, and two more creatures go down, their large craniums stitched with black scorches that have penetrated deep. Indeed, these are more than just scorching wounds, for their brows are furrowed in the extreme. Brain tissue has been burned away, and the wounds cauterized. When Major Octavia looks at the wounds Tiger has inflicted she has to wonder how Tiger managed to cause so much damage.

"So that's what the *overcharge* setting does," Tiger comments, and then she says: "Major, I think my weapon's power supply is burned out."

"No, just depleted. It doesn't matter though, I'm pretty sure we got them all," says Major Octavia.

"Are you sure? We haven't penetrated this structure enough to even know what it may have been," Tiger responds.

"I'm fairly certain at one time this was a command and control platform, literally the flag ship for a fleet admiral," says the Major.

"What would we ever do with that?" asks Tiger.

A *thing* leaps past me, screaming as it goes, and from the volume of sound I hear the *thing* must have brought its whole family of screamers along with. I start shooting almost instantly. I find my targets first, and then I shoot. Horrors in the shadows, I stitch them with shots from the electro-rifle, and it only makes the screaming worse. The things try to close the distance. They want intimacy. It seems they can only kill up close, and I do everything I can to deny them what they desire. I can hear Green fighting nearby, her weapon fire precise, utmost effective, and for every critter that gets by me, I know Green has scores a kill. I'm probably down on points, and it will cost me my life. I shoot and shoot, yet the creepy things keep coming, they keep screaming, and I fear that even if I should live through this, my ears will have suffered permanent damage for all the screaming these things emit. They must have throats like brass instruments. Just as the thought of how much charge is left to the power pack my weapon relies upon, the thing fizzles. The sound it makes is a literal *fizzle* and then one of the *things* is in front of me. It slaps my weapon aside, and then slaps me to the floor. Before this moment I never imagined anything so strong as to have the ability to knock my off my feet with a single blow. If you didn't know, then take my word for it: I can take a punch and right to the face, when I have to. Yet the trick it to land the punches yourself, to hit them in the face, just as a great leader once said: you may have to die for your country, only the smart soldier gets the enemy to die for their country. While I may now be a mercenary, a soldier without a country, that doesn't change the fact that I would rather my enemies die for their country, or at least be the ones who take all the punches to the face. Either way, at the moment I know I must now fight with my hands. This thought fills my head, penetrating the fog that's set in because of the blow I suffered. I have to fight now, and with every tool I have at my disposal. I try to move; I try to reclaim my footing except the creature has a hold of me, lifting me up and off of my feet. For real, my toes don't touch the ground for how high the creature has raised me. This delay will cost my assailant, because as the monster attempts to throw me back down onto the hard deck, I spring into motion. I manage to get one of the creature's limbs extended and twisted along one side of my body as I fall and as I hit the deck the limb snaps, breaking at one point, and dislocating at one of the joints. The creature is screaming again, except now the screams are from pain, a level of agony the monster never imagined possible. I almost take pause, because in my hands I have the end of that creature's ruined limb, and I'm not sure if I'm holding a hand, or a claw, or some kind of pincer? Either way, I know I have to transition to another position, because that's the best way to control the fight. Now that I have the control I am dodging when the monster tries to bite me with a kind of mandible-jaw that makes me cry out in fear when I see it almost get me. It may not have been the best form of retaliation, however it was effective when I rammed one booted foot into its mouth and then rolled away backwards. Then I extended my hands in hopes of recovering my weapon, thinking it might have recycled the power charge. If only there were some light here. A matt black weapon is hard to see against the kind of darkness that pervades this derelict vessel. Then there is a flash, stillness, and a silence that seems all too pervasive. I turn my head to look, and standing down the corridor is my Lieutenant Green, stock to shoulder, and a regenerating charge indicator on the side of her weapon.

"You saved my life," I tell her.

"No, I just cut short another of your knock down, and drag out brawls," says Green, and her teeth seem to shine in the dark. The girl does have a lovely smile, all the more so does it seem so when she is the one to have just killed the thing that was trying to kill you. "I think that was the end of them, as if they all came here, just for us," Green comments as she looks about at the bodies covering the deck.

"That's just the way it would play out, Tiger and the Major have probably been sorting through a galley, and finding all kinds of gourmet rations that are still ready to go, while we are stuck here killing an entire hive's worth of warrior drones. There's probably more on the way, this can't be the entire generation of those things. I would wager the Major is eating beef tips in the creamiest gravy imaginable at the moment, while we probably have at least another half dozen of these things yet to kill," I say, and yes, I did sound a good mix of sarcastic and bitter. That's called caustic, right? Maybe? Another word I've got to look up.

"Actually that half dozen killer drones were the welcoming party that received us," a voice calls over the radio. It's the Major's voice, and I cringe realizing she's heard what I have been saying. Yet she doesn't deliver me any reprimand, she says nothing of my insubordination. Major Octavia only gives us a set of coordinates to follow for rendezvous. This inevitably leads to us coming upon more of the infestation. The ones we encountered initially must have been the true soldiers, the hive shock troops and blitz-style defenders. I say that because every drone creature we later encounter is slower, and they seem to have a purely self-defensive response to their nature. It's almost as if we could have walked by them and suffered no harm if we never took a posture that presented any kind of threat. Yet we have our orders, the infestation is to be cleared out, no exceptions. If this true alien species we have encountered is capable of producing those same shock troops we originally faced, then I can understand the decision to wipe them out. How many drones do we kill on the way to the rendezvous? About four each, or something like that, I am sure. I am considering asking the Major about the heavy handedness of how we are dealing with the xeno-morphs, when I hear her in conversation with Tiger, and what I overhear answers my question for me.

"Oh, several samples of the aliens were already collected for replication, manipulation and modification, whatever suits the Widow. She has staff for that sort of thing, and I hear she has a man who can work wonders in the realm. She just doesn't call on him that often. Something about the past still causing tension in their relationship," Major Octavia is heard to be telling Tiger as we enter the compartment.

The compartment itself is big, just outright huge, and the number of people working here is mindboggling. I don't know if the command and control space of the *Impervious* was nearly this big, and that was the largest battle wagon I have ever ridden. Well, it was the only battleship I've ever seen. I am a soldier, not a sailor, so I see shipboard travel only by necessity. I have no idea what happens on a *pleasure cruise*. Don't feel bad for me or any of the rest of the soldier-girls, we've gotten to see some fine vacation time recently, the benefit of pleasing a wealthy patron.

The space we find ourselves in now is just astounding, and for a moment I feel like I'm having trouble seeing from one end to the other. Yet what is most curious is the very center of the space. What I see there is surely the heart of some manner of command and control system. Except I cannot imagine how this one might work because the seating is only for two people, and the plush command couches face away from each other. Who does that? What sort of efficiency could that possibly facilitate? Just as these thoughts are running through my mind one of the chief technicians working here walks up, and as he stands just behind me, he says: "It's really amazing."

"What is?" I am quick to ask.

"That we were given a full suit *Janus* command and control console, the latest model even. Add to that the fact that we were given the support necessary to make it work perfectly," he tells me.

This is when two distinctly odd things happen. First I notice Lieutenant Green standing directly opposite my position. She's looking over the strange console just as I have been, and in fact she seems more perplexed than I am about it, or perhaps she apprehends the situation better than do I. Also this is when Major Octavia takes note of our behavior.

"Commander Black, egress time! Dust off your team and get them back to the boat. We have places to be, and the boss lady to see, so get your team moving, *now*," Major Octavia orders, and I hear the bark in her voice as she speaks the last word.

I don't think too much about it. Although her sudden, and stern commands garner a large number of stares from the host of engineers and technicians present, no one questions the Major's expulsion of her soldier-girls from what it seems will be the command bridge of the improvised battle station they are *attempting* to make from the *Void-Helkein*.

Chapter Four

At least I *thought* we would be leaving.

As soon as we got back to the *Dowager's Daughter* the Major was on the horn demanding we send the prisoner down the line. For what, she did not say and it was a long hour before we could form any kind of educated guess. We put the poor woman into the rigging necessary to send her down from the Dowager's Daughter to the Void Helkein and then she was on her way. Truth is, I felt sorry for her because God only knows what the Major was going to do to her while she had the chance, without anyone watching that is. An hour elapsed, and we saw a torpedo launched from the Void-Helkein. The weapon emerged at a really bizarre angle from some part of the enormous thing we surely hadn't seen at all until just now. None of us Soldier-Girls knew what to make of it, yet I heard Captain Malloy mutter in amazement. He turned on a speaker, and the radio chatter was incomprehensible, at least it was to me.

"That is some pretty amazing false broadcasting. I bet it would even fool the Arcadians themselves," he says, his voice very quiet, just above a whisper. Then he looks at the rest of us, and he says: "You know there is only one person who could have pulled this off." He says this with a wink of an eye.

"Who?" asks White, and the Captain gives her a long look of pity. So I am glad it was another who asked when I was wondering just the same thing.

The torpedo is flying fast, and is about to disappear into the dark of the void when there is a flash of light and the torpedo has disappeared. Captain Malloy begins to swipe his fingers over display screens, looking at numbers, viewing some graphs and other charts, and then he looks at us again, saying: "You know that torpedo was modified, right? You know it wasn't a message torpedo, and while it wasn't carrying a warhead, it was carrying a message, right?"

Green and Tiger are frowning at him. White is all wide-eyed, and I would be also, except I have a much better poker face. Strange that, because I've never been any good at poker, or chess, the abstracts always seem to elude me.

Captain Malloy stares at us for a few long moments, and then he asks what I'm sure he thinks is a simple question: "How many of you think that prisoner will ever be coming back?"

At least two of us Soldier-Girls are looking at him with profound confusion. White raises a hand before she asks: "What are you getting at, Captain?"

"I don't know. I'm like the rest of you: I will never know the whole truth of what we do. Yet what I can tell you is this: the torpedo was reconfigured to carry a message, a literal broadcast message, and I'm fairly certain the prisoner was placed inside the warhead section of the torpedo with some minimal form of life support, just to reinforce the message. They must have reconfigured the whole torpedo. Instead of a targeting system, they installed a navigation system. Instead of a warhead and detonation mechanism they installed a lifeboat style compartment and placed that woman inside. They surely removed the weapon style propulsion system and installed a long range shuttle system. Now the torpedo has been sent toward Bellazar controlled space broadcasting on known Bellazar frequencies, and the codes I saw I am very certain are current for both their military and diplomatic channels. God only knows what's being told to the Bellazars, and I would guess there is an outside chance the message is actually intended to be intercepted by the Arcadians. What do they call that, a false flag operation? Or is it simply referred to as *disinformation*?" asks Captain Malloy.

All of us Soldier-Girls hear him out, yet that's all he gets. After listening to the Captain, Green and Tiger have clearly become disinterested. They desire other employment. White is actually looking sad for some reason I can't imagine, and I dread exploring because you know, mushy feelings and all that. I decide we have been standing around here long enough, and because there are actual chores to do, I start to give orders. "Right, we have weapons and other gear that need to be stowed, and need maintenance first, so let's get to it people, pronto," I tell my Soldier-Girls and we are all off, headed back to the ship's armory. Green and Tiger lead the way, and that allows me to walk with my girl, White. "So, what's it?" I ask of her.

"Commander?" she replies.

"Tell us what's bothering you, because you can't lie, I know you are bothered," I say to her.

"Is the Major going to get Irwin killed?" she asks, and I can hear the distress in her voice.

"He isn't even about, so how could she get him killed?" I ask her, mostly to settle her agitated feelings.

"Irwin gets drawn into these crazy things we do. The Widow pulls him into her plots, and they are always dangerous, or else she wouldn't need us. Irwin doesn't know how to fight. He doesn't know when he needs to hide. If he gets too involved in dangerous stuff then he will get killed," White tells me in response to the question I shouldn't have asked. No one I know can expound on problems I don't want to hear about the way my girl White can, and she does it every time I ask. If only I would remember to stop asking.

"Irwin is a full grown man. He makes his own decisions, and no one can stop that, so if he walks down the wrong dark alley, whatever happens will happen. You can't protect him. You can't stop his life from happening," I tell her, in the hopes I've come up with some good advice.

"I want to stop all the bad things from happening to him. I don't want him walking down dark alleys. I want to protect him. I want to be there always to protect him, because when I worry about him it hurts, right here," she says to me, and she is actually pointing toward the heart.

'Aw gawd, what is this, some women's home cinema of the week?' I'm thinking. I have to keep myself from rolling my eyes. I have to stop myself from telling her that she is talking like some overly emotional woman. Except she's in love with this stupid, rich, fat man, and there is not a thing I can do about it. The bizarre idiot managed to win the heart of my girl, and now I have to listen to her babble and then wipe her tears every time she thinks he might stub a toe, or prick a finger. I swear to God, Irwin Grossman, if you break her heart, I will kill you, slow, painful, and terrible, that is sure, I will kill you.

Then we are in the armory, doing maintenance checks on all the gear and weapons we used. We were working in silence, getting things done, and stowing the gear all proper, until we heard something we weren't supposed to ever hear.

"She's going to be insane," we hear Captain Malloy say over the intercom. They left the channel open, or more likely the Captain was trying to ease drop on us while we were down in his armory, and then he forgot to kill the cannel when the Major returned to the ship and walked in on him while he was on the bridge plotting our course home.

"We can't be afraid of her," says the Major. We all stand still as statuary, listening to the verboten verbal exchange.

"Well, she *can* fire us. You don't want to be out of a job, do you?" the Captain asks.

"I can always find work, it is just that I would prefer not to need a new employer," the Major replies.

"She got me back on my feet. She pulled me out of the gutter. I owe her," says the Captain.

"She got the project started, and trust me when I say you are in recovery, a true work in progress. You need to bear in mind that she sent people to pull you out of the gutter. She had other people do the work of keeping you clean, or as clean as could be managed. Essentially she farmed out the work to her staff, at least one of whom she had failed to vet properly and then blamed you for the failure," says the Major.

"I thought it was you who found the spy, and then told her it was my fault she had a spy in her network?" asks the Captain.

"A bit of side *a*, and then a smidgen from column *two*, you can never be sure," says the Major.

"I think I can tell now when you are being evasive," we hear the Captain tell her, and for a moment it feels like I can *hear* a smile in his voice. Yet such is impossible.

"That just means we are synchronized, working together all proper like," she responds, and what we hear next sounds very strange. Some odd noises come across the line, and it goes on for a few long moments until we hear the Major ask: "Why is the intercom line open?"

That's when we hear a click, the channel is closed, and I look around at my people. They need to get back to work, and we need to get someplace out of sight. Yet the actual chore is still far from complete. The weapons all have to be cleared. The respiration helmets need to be reset before they can be used again. The tasks are piled, and they drag out. We are still working when the Major steps into the armory and she is looking at us. She isn't angry, yet her face is hard set. At least it isn't anger. She's just looking at us, and after a few moments she simply says: "I suppose we all have a private life to some extent, and then those moments come when what was private becomes public. It would be stupid to try and just pretend none of you were listening."

"We didn't know what to do, we just started hearing voices," White tells her.

"And none of you have ever really been able to enjoy a premium level of privacy," the Major responds.

"I have been with them, always, all of my life," I say, looking back over my shoulder at all of my girls.

"I want all of you to know that I need you. I will need you always. For what is coming I will need you, and you should never forget it," the Major tells us.

"You mean when you and the Captain have your talk with the Widow?" asks Tiger, as speculation.

"No, I mean for what's to come after. I don't want to say that what we will be facing will be a greater challenge than we have ever seen before, I am only sure that the danger will be great. I can't tell you everything now, because the brief is not fully unpacked. We can't do that yet. However what I can say is that where we are going will be frontier territory, wild and untamed. Morganti will have us stepping on toes hard just as she always does, and you know that doesn't make people happy, just remember it usually leads to some good ends, or at least better than any of us individually can envision," says the Major.

I turn again, giving each of my Soldier-Girls a look in the eye, and then I turn back to the Major, saying: "We are with you."

"Good, then get to the crash couches because we are doing a hard jump, with hot course," she tells us, and we begin to scramble. Everyone knows to be strapped in whenever the Major or Captain Malloy use phrases like *'hard jump'* or *'hot course'*. It is all actually very simple to explain. The Captain and his crew have over clocked the FTL drive, that is to say they have accelerated the natural safe capabilities of the Faster than Light engines. Let us say the *Dowager's Daughter* typically, safely, goes five hundred times the speed of light to make intergalactic travel a feasible thing. If we are doing a *Hard Jump* then the ship will be going at least a thousand times faster than the speed of light. As for the Hot Course, I think that refers to a navigational trick the Captain is attempting that is the equivalent of taking shortcuts. To use another idiom, we are *cutting corners* in an intensive effort to get home quicker, and to think about it, that is sad, because we are only going to be heading out again as fast as possible. Even sadder is the fact that our Major and Captain, they will probably be getting intensively reprimanded for what is entirely a personal matter.

Anyway, we all get into crash couches, we strap in, and then we spend three hours under red lights that are not part of the ship's lighting system. So where all the red light comes from I don't know. Also there is a feeling that we are doing something wrong, like we are being allowed to break the rules, even as the watchman has us under his eye. I might have fallen asleep during the transition, or I might have just been hypnotized by the horrid, unnatural light and the shrill keening that varied in volume the whole time we were in *Hot Jump* or whatever Captain Malloy calls it. Either way it is White who pats my face to wake me when the ship has resumed normal space flight. The Major stands there nearby, and she is looking stern, because that's her job.

"Is she harmed?" the Major asks.

"No, it looks to be just a minor fatigue related reaction. Except Commander Black was only in a shoot-out on the *Void-Helkein* just like the rest of you so I don't know what the additional stress factor could be the cause of this," White comments.

"She had to fight one of them hand-to-hand, remember?" says Green.

"One of the xeno-morphs, she fought one of those things all by herself?" asks the Major.

Did she forget, or did I fail to report properly? Either way the Major gets an odd look on her face, which is hard to discern because of her ever present dark glasses and she is casting her gaze about, looking at everyone. She looks at all of us soldier-girls. Then she is looking at the chief of the boat, and the deckhands. Lastly she is looking at Captain Malloy who has come down from the bridge to see what the fuss is about. It's about nothing, they just need to let me get to my feet and walk it off.

"We are at station keeping, and ready to make atmospheric entry, unless you want to wait," Captain Malloy says to the Major. Then the most bizarre thing I have seen and heard in the longest time happens. The Major turns away from everyone. She appears to be headed for the galley.

"No, now we have special meal time, and then we will return to our duties," says Major Octavia.

I am perplexed by what happened after that announcement. You see we were all assigned tasks that were not necessarily part of the plan of the day we were following. The Major took White aside at first, and then after some secret plotting on their part, (everything with the Major is a secret plot), White then came back to us with job assignments for everyone. She took several moments reminding us of her role as morale and logistics officer before doling out the new tasking. (If White is my logistics officer, why is it always someone else who inventories and orders ammunition?) I thought I would be called to the kitchen, instead I was sent to the cargo bay. The Chief of the Boat, another deck hand, and I, we worked at creating the most attractive table we could manage. We set out a long white table, and dressed it with white tissue paper as the table cloth. It was a white theme you could say because we then set out white disposable plates and flatware. "White floral centerpieces are all that is needed, and yet we don't have," the Chief says, and for a moment I question his manhood, only in my thoughts though. And what was it with that smile he wore every moment we were working side by side? The drinking cups were of clear plastic, so we didn't manage an all-white theme. The Major actually took Tiger with her into the galley, along with the one deckhand that usually did all the cooking on board. From what I heard they spent the next long stretch of time tinkering with something called a *pressure cooker*. I didn't find out until later what Green was assigned to do.

We sat for our meal. It turned out the Major had Tiger keeping something in the freezer called *squirrel*, and it was something the Major told us she remembered with unshakable fondness from her childhood. We were eating a thick stew of squirrel, potatoes and carrots. It was so rich I thought it must be fattier than whale meat. Yes, I have in my lifetime been able to sample both the meat and the blubber from whale, and it was good stuff I will say. Yet the meal was odd for us soldier girls, seeing how we can consume foods, yet we also can go long periods, nearly indefinitely without consuming food stuffs. We eat when we need, and that is not often, or we eat when the desire comes upon us, and that is not often. We are machine people, modified only once since we entered the service of the Widow, and her principle agent: Major Octavia. The absence of an obedience chip, a processor that compelled our submission, in one form or another, still troubles us. The removal of said processor was the great gift of Morganti, and yet it was probably done to make us see her with such loyalty as to rival our previous masters, who were also our builders, not creators mind you, only our builders. The difference between a builder and a creator is probably too great a lesson for me to give you in what little space I possess here.

Let me say this: I am talking about the difference between *the Creator*, and the men who have built something, anything. By my perspective a design engineer, an inventive scientist, and the technicians that fabricate and then assemble what they call for are nothing compared to what I mean when I say *the Creator*. This is just the same as when I tell you that an architect, carpenters and masons are nothing compared to *the Creator*. I exist because of a *Creator*. Now see what you have done? You dragged me off onto a tangent. It's all your fault, don't try to deny it. What was I saying?

We have sat for a meal. It feels special, and good, and everyone seems to smile, every one of us. We sip fizzy drink from the plastic cups. We eat the stew, as thick as it is we still eat it, every bite, it's that good. Most of us have a second helping. White and Tiger have a third helping. The Major barely finishes her one plate even though it appears now she was planning just this special meal for so long the meat had to be placed in deep freeze. There is laughter. The Chief and his deckhands, all the boys make jokes and all the girls laugh. At one moment I catch sight of the Major and the Captain holding hands, at least until they realize they are doing so in a very public way. It shouldn't matter, not anymore. Anyone who has seen them together knew they were on track to a beautiful love affair, or a murder and suicide of some form. White nearly takes a third helping until Tiger reminds her of our constant necessity to be *mission ready*. It's a thin contrivance, yet necessary. No unit needs a fat medic, sleepy of eye from overeating.

This is when I begin to think it's time to clean up when I hear the Major speaking.

"Lieutenant, I believe you were going to share a song with us, before our meal was done?" asks Octavia. Lieutenant stands before she speaks.

"Yes I am, just as you asked. This is prescient, and of value, not just because this is our first formal, and special meal together, also because any meal we have could be our last, though let's not dwell on that thought. We did not say grace, and so that is another reason the song the Major asked me to sing is valuable. So I offer this: a classic that has changed little over the centuries since it was first composed," announces the Lieutenant. With only a little more delay, she begins to sing.

"The Amazing Grace, so sweet a sound
That's saved the wretched me!
I was lost for so long, yet now I am found
I was Blind, yet now allowed to see.

It was Grace that gave my heart fear
And by Grace my fears cast away.
How precious was that moment
When grace first appeared!
How precious was that hour
When I first believed!

Through dangers, toils, and traps
I have come so far.
It is Grace that has brought me through
And Grace that calls me Home.

My Lord, His promise is good to me,
His Word secures all my hope.
My shield and succor my Lord be
As long as life's in me.

My flesh and heart shall fail,
And this mortal shell will cease.
I shall pass beyond the veil,
To know a life of joy and peace.

The Earth we'll see crumble to dust,
And the sun will go dark.
Yet God who called to me
I will forever rest in thee."

I sit there shocked. I didn't know she had it in her. Or I am at least caught off guard by the power of her performance. I think she put something extra into the performance, something that I and the other soldier girls never before heard? Either way, Tiger, White, and I, we three sit there jaws agape, and eyes wide. All the others begin a modest round of applause while the closest companions and truest family Green has? We sit there, looking like idiots because she has done something that's surprised us. She put her heart, her soul, all her spirit into the song, and managed a perfect performance. She seemed to bring additional life to the lyrics, lifting the words and phrases, and I am sure it was not her spirit alone that achieved this feat.

I'm trying to think of something to say. I'm her Commander. When Green does something worthy of commendation, then I should be the first one speak up. Yet we soldier girls, when presented with this moment that at the very least is commendable, we sit like idiots who have looked Medusa in the eye. Before the Gorgon we have become statuary. It is the Major who honors our comrade. Octavia stands, she goes to my Lieutenant Green to embrace and commend, and congratulate.

"You did so well that your own sisters are speechless. I would say take pride in that, yet I know to whom you give all the glory, the one you cast your crowns to, and I encourage it wholly," Octavia says, and she does so with the biggest smile I've ever seen her wear with any of us. She's never once smiled like that for me, with me, at me, and I am so jealous. My envy is probably beyond my comprehension, because while I don't realize its manifestation, at least one person present does. Really I just have no idea what to do or say. *Something* else does the speaking instead.

"Auto-Pilot engaged, orbital pattern eminent, input for any landing or modified maneuvers required," announces a synthesized voice.

"What's that?" demands Tiger.

"The auto-pilot, just like it said," Captain Malloy tells her.

"You've never used it before that any of us know. I wouldn't have even thought this ship was equipped," Tiger responds.

"The ship is under equipped in at least a few aspects, very certainly," Captain Malloy replies, without delving into what those deficits of equipment actually may be. At least he's not smiling about it. The man far too often has an idiot's sense of humor about things everyone else considers terrifyingly serious.

"Why are you using the automatic pilot now when you have never used it before?" asks Tiger.

"I use it all the time. You've notice only once. I'm using it now because this was our special time together. You don't want anything ordinary, anything boorish to interrupt your special family meal," Captain Malloy tells her, and we are all left in silence, again. It was like the air left the room when he used the word *family*. That awful old drunk Jack Malloy, he thinks of us as *his family*. Well, he has rushed in several times to save our lives. "Now excuse me, I have to land this rig," he says and then the Captain is gone.

Not just the Captain leaves. The deckhands swing into action. The Major has commands flying off the tip of her tongue. Everything has changed, and the odd truth of the matter is that all of this is because we have come back home. The not so odd thing is this: we may never return again. Our jobs are dangerous.

The *Dowager's Daughter* lands, and ground crew quickly get to work, swarming over the skin of the vessel, and invading the ship's interior. They are clearly on a schedule, and this fills me with foreboding. We are on a quick turnaround, and I have to question why we even came all the way back here if Morganti wants us in the field so badly.

We all climb into a chartered bus that was apparently booked for five, because when Captain Malloy begins to board, the driver says: "I was told it was only ladies."

"One more doesn't change anything, and I'm going to the exact same place as the ladies," Captain Malloy responds.

Tiger giggles, and she leans over, saying to the rest of us: "They called us *ladies*."

"Mistakes are bound to happen," I comment, eyes front as if addressing no one in particular.

"If we behave like ladies we will be treated like ladies," says Green, very stiff of both neck and lip.

This is a moment where I am sure either Tiger or White are sure to get mouthy, and when White begins to open her mouth, I dread what's to come out. Yet I also see Tiger pinch White upon the thigh as she whispers: "Do not say a thing."

White shuts her mouth, and we ride in peace. The only other contact the whole way is when I spy the Captain placing his hand atop the Major's. I expect her to pull away, and yet I get the feeling she's taking comfort in the gesture.

We arrive at the big house, the Widow's home, and just like any time before, it seems massive, imposing, and representative of more wealth than I could ever comprehend. Of course I am a poor soldier who has nothing.

Inside we are greeted by the Widow herself, and if you didn't know, I here swear to you that this is most unusual. She didn't answer her own door, nothing insane as that, yet she was there, seated and ready when we were shown in. At all other times Morganti always keeps people waiting. She is never there when you arrive. At best she is in her solon, or atrium when you show up, and you are kept waiting outside while her hired man checks in to see if it is permissible to show you in. No, this time we are taken straight into the solon where Morganti, the Widow of Market Town stands waiting for us. *She* is *waiting* for us, and she's dressed different. I don't care about any apocryphal stories you may have heard about Morganti greeting people in white lingerie so lacy you would think it impossible. I respect the woman, so to me those stories have little credence, even if it is the Major who is the principle source of the stories. Morganti set me free. I am forever in her debt. For this meeting she is not in lace or lingerie, she is in her business suit, and yet not as she has been before. Morganti has her first four buttons undone. The Widow is showing off lots of cleavage. What is she trying to do? *What statement is she trying to make?* What is this discordance, the wearing of a conservative suit, yet so provocatively? Why not confirm the old stories and show up for the business meeting in silk camisole?

I realize Morganti is only looking at two people: Captain Jack, and Major Octavia. She isn't just looking at them, she is glaring at them. Is there something in the history here that I am unaware of? The harsh stare only becomes worse when Morganti allows her gaze to fall and she sees that Jack and Octavia have once more taken each other by the hand. Yet what Morganti says is entirely on a different subject.

"The transmissions you have sent have been invaluable. You have made it possible to set into motion an operation that was previously thought to be nearly impossible. Because of the intelligence provided in your dispatches we can begin to move against rival parties. What was before only a remotely possible advance, has taken on the form of a genuine coup that is almost sure to happen, and it is because of you, Major, and your people," Morganti tells us. Well, she is mostly speaking to Octavia, yet I am sure you knew that. Also, when she says *'and your people'* I can distinctly hear the tone of afterthought. Morganti is distracted, and we all know what distracts her. Finally she gets around to voicing what troubles her: "So, the two of you, in spite of the totality of *history*."

The Captain is looking stern, and I am sure he wants to say something, yet he holds his peace.

Morganti begins to walk their way. She comes to a stop when she is standing just before Captain Malloy. Is she presenting her cleavage? What is happening here?

"New navigational information is to be found on the ship?" asks the Captain.

"Have I ever before left you waning, dearest Jack?" she asks, a warm purr conveyed by her voice.

"Our new mission brief, has it been transmitted as well?" asks Major Octavia. For daring to speak up, the Major earns herself what I am sure was intended as a withering stare. The Major endures.

"The navigational plan is being loaded to your ship as we speak. Your tactical brief is awaiting you, ready to display from a closed device that for security purposes is locked *read only*. You will have everything you need, yet as always: study well," Morganti tells the Major, meeting her eye to eye in what at first seems to be an attempted stare down. Morganti forgot the Major has her dark glasses on. How can she have forgotten? The Major always has her dark glasses on. Perhaps Morganti can't stop herself? Moments go by until one of them speaks.

"Proper preparation and planning prevent pathetic performance," Major Octavia seems to recite to the Widow.

"You borrowed those wise words," Morganti is quick to say.

"Borrowed from one of the best, and I paraphrase," the Major replies, yet by now Morganti has completely turned her attention to Captain Malloy.

"So, you are set on your present course?" she asks.

"I admit the detour is most unexpected, yet I have you to thank for opening the way," the Captain tells her. I don't know if anyone understands what he is talking about. I don't see comprehension on the face of anyone else in the room. Morganti seems to apprehend him, somehow, or in some way. The Major's face is unreadable, yet *unreadable* is her natural state.

"Get out," Morganti says of a sudden and no one wants to respond.

"What?" Captain Malloy asks before anyone can even move.

The look Morganti gives him could wither red woods. A moment passes before any other sort of sound can be heard, and then it is the Widow speaking again: "Dismissed."

Part Two
Live and on Tour!

Chapter Five

"I don't even know where we are going."

"I ah, I believe it was made very clear, sir," Gomer Mosley responds with the affectation of a smile, even while his head twitches with nervous anxiety.

Yandi Yodel gives Gomer a look. Yandi isn't sure what to make of Gomer, other than he finds this man to be a very odd character.

"Did you read the dossier?" asks Valeria Hogan, sounding both serious and overly cheerful.

"You need to read the dossier," Nelly Silver is quick to add, sounding both stern and happy to be helpful.

Yandi give the women an irritated look. He's taken no comfort in these *so-called* 'operatives' that Gomer and Excelentia Excalibur Excidium have insisted they bring along. Well, Gomer insisted, and Excelentia supported him in what seemed to be a *by rote* fashion.

"We told you, repeatedly, our destination is *Aborto Espontáneo Blanco*. You actually own the whole planet," Excelentia reminds Yandi, and the undercurrent of exasperation is clear to be heard in her voice.

"That guy never actually told me his name," Yandi comments.

"A stranger on the street, some odd character you were only briefly to meet?" asks Tanya Petite, her smile accompanied by vacant eyes that leave Yandi wondering what she may be looking at.

"Surely someone he knew, a person of importance, an old acquaintance, and not anyone new," says Pricilla Hogan, as if reciting lines of verse.

Yandi looks in the direction of Tanya and Pricilla, and he's thinking they couldn't be anymore strange. No, he's thinking they couldn't be any more disturbing. He's never seen people so disconcerting by their presence. By his reckoning something is very wrong with the four operatives that Gomer calls *Xavier's Seraphim*. "The notion of one man owning an entire planet seems fantastic," Yandi eventually comments, and then he goes on: "That man I met at your offices, I never actually got his name. He wasn't Xavier Gosling, and Gomer, you don't act like he was your boss, so who the heck was he? You are taking me to a planet you say I own after I somehow negotiated your services with a man whose name I never learned."

"The, ah, the concept, legally speaking, the doctrine under the law, that is to say, the concept is still under review, as some would say, while others of much more sounder thinking, clearly they affirm such a notion of property rights, in their... how to put it, in their sound wisdom, and put forth the theory," Gomer Mosley tries to explain, his facial tics and twitches nearly out of control.

"Pricilla, did the brief say anything about this case moving through the courts?" asks Valeria Hogan, looking at her sister with undeniable concern.

"Don't you remember, silly? The brief talked about the stalwart natives who need to be relocated, or liquidated, for progress," says Pricilla, an overly effusive smile on her face.

"You are talking about Aborto Espontáneo Blanco? The planet has a native population that refuses to recognize the land claims of the Ignis Corporate Group?" asks Yandi, himself sounding very troubled by the thought.

"It doesn't matter what they recognize! Their Queen signed the treaty, she agreed to her compensation package, and she has received her payment! Any tribal people who resist the progressive wave need to be wiped away, not allowed to air their grievances! You know that's what Jasper Ignis would have done!" Excelentia is quick to say, and she's nearly shouting. Yet she is trying to pilot the luxury yacht they travel within on this interstellar journey.

"She's agitated," says Nelly Silver, looking very concerned, with a not too subtle a frown.

"From the emotional damage she suffered while a member of that mind control cult," responds Tanya Petite with a knowing nod of her head, though her eyes still clearly vacant.

"There's a Queen? We are going to meet this Queen?" asks Yandi, his face writ with confusion.

"He didn't read the brief," says Nelly Silver, with a shake of her head and a frown.

"He most definitely didn't read the brief," says Pricilla Hogan, pity in her voice and the expression on her face.

"Meet with her is an understatement, a... ah, what I'm telling you, that is, what must be said, in advance mind you, is its a few feet short of the whole yard. What I'm trying to explain is this: we are on our way to a very important *meeting* with

Empress Semiramis. We're going to have an *unquestionably* vital talk with the old gal. She may be on the fence, undecided on the issues, so to speak, yet if we can bring her around, then the tribal leaders will have no choice about falling into line. That is to say: once we solidify the Queen's position, we will bring an end to any upstart rebellion among the tribal leaders," Gomer Mosley explains.

"Carpet bombs," says Valeria Hogan.

"High yield incendiary munitions," says Tanya Petite.

"Nerve gas delivered in clusters," says Nelly Silver.

"Children's toys and household goods infested with weaponized and virulent pathogens," says Pricilla Hogan.

Each woman as she speaks has a hard set blank look on her face.

"What are they talking about?" Yandi asks Excelentia.

"That's just a game they play, it's like they are brainstorming, to solve problems in advance," Excelentia replies. She doesn't meet him by the eye.

From the time they arrive on the planet Aborto Espontáneo Blanco, to their presentation before the Empress Semiramis, the time seems to rush by for Yandi Yodel. The place is primitive, and the people are not much more than hunter/gatherers at best. When Excelentia lands the yacht, she is setting down in a clearing that looks recent, and made entirely with hand tools. Yet the landing is without difficulty, and thus of no added stress. As they disembark the yacht a cordon of warriors is there to escort Yandi and his party to the queen's court.

Yandi nearly falls into a state of shock as he is entering the throne room of Empress Semiramis. The scene is motley, so very much so, and his eyes move about slowly taking in the sight of many varied hunting trophies, uncountable animal skins stretched for display, and exotic tree bark as wall hangings with of course carvings in both wood and bone hung as decorations. The wood carvings hung up appear mostly to be weapons and shields, yet there are also tools, possibly smoking pipes? And there are feathers. The animal skins are fewer than the reptile skins, and while the feathers are fewer than the animal skins, the feathers seem quite conspicuous in their display, as if you are supposed to notice them. Yandi determines an order of precedence: reptile skins at the bottom, then animal skin, and at the very top the apex are the feathers. Also, the figure sitting central to all of the actions and events in this, the throne room supposedly of all Aborto Espontáneo Blanco, is wearing a copious amount, and even gaudy display of feathers. This is the Empress Semiramis, the self-declared ruler of Aborto Espontáneo Blanco, the self-identified unifying queen of all the tribes and nations of what is an abundantly lush planet, yet possibly the home of mostly very primitive peoples. The notion of the people here being *primitive* is supported by the appearance of their queen at court: she's nearly half naked as she sits giving her people and these otherworldly visitors audience. Empress Semiramis is clothed, or at least she is covered. Her headdress alone is composed of over a thousand feathers befitting her station as a wealthy royal. Her bosom and loins are dressed in furs, lush white fur that to Yandi seem akin to ermine, or mink. As Yandi looks around the royal chamber he notices the divisions. The most noble persons present wear feathers, not nearly as many feathers as the Empress, yet they wear a number of feathers. These notable nobles also wear leather, animal skins, if not furs. As Yandi scans the mass of people he intentionally looks for those who might be menials, or those who might be from the lowest classes. After scanning the entirety of the crowd Yandi sees the pattern, and he realizes he should have seen it earlier. The number of feathers a noble wears is relative to their proximity to the Empress. The third of the room closest to the Empress is crowded with high ranking nobles wearing feathers and furs. The middle third of the royal chamber is more densely packed, and most of those people wear only a few feathers, and their furs are of low quality. The back of the throne room near the entrance is where people are forced to stand in contact so tightly in proximity to each other. These are the poor folks, the retched refuse, and they mostly wear reptile skins. Indeed, the ones here who may have come into some minor wealth in their lifetimes, they wear better quality leathers. Yet because they are all poor here in the back of the royal chamber, not a one of them wears fur or feathers. Because they are here for audience with their queen, they are in the best reptile skins they can afford. The one constant, all of them are pretty much half naked, blue skinned aliens. Now Yandi Yodel looks down at the ridiculous costume he's put on and understands.

While they were still on the yacht, yet long after the ship had set down and was secure, Excelentia had come to Yandi and made him take off all his clothes that the garments might be exchanged for what Yandi considered a ridiculous headdress of feathers, as well as a shirt and kilt of tawny fur. The shirt was fringed with feathers along the sleeves and the bottom. The kilt was festooned with what seemed to Yandi like round badges affixed with numerous fine feathers. Yandi knew nothing about fashion or what the best feather dressing for your clothing could be, yet he had a sense that Excelentia has gone out of her way to buy the best feathers available for this lunatic costume she convinced him to wear. The only reason he put it on: he was meeting a Queen.

Empress Semiramis looks out over her subjects, petitioners, and all gathered here before her grandeur. While she tries to let it be seen that she's looking closely at all the visitors, the queen is most closely evaluating the strangers. The off world visitors, they seem like low peasants to her, all of them, because they are dressed in the lowest form of adornment possible, natural fibers, woven fabrics. On this beautiful planet ruled by the Empress Samiramis, mostly lunatics, the hopelessly impoverished, and the wretchedly ignorant are the only ones who wear *cloth*, made from cotton or wool. Before the coming of outsiders, or any other-worlders, no one even knew to call the clothes of the poor and insane *cotton* or *wool*. Now people even speak of natural fibers they call silk and something else they call *synthetic*. They talk about the spinning of threads and weaving of cloth as if it were a natural act. The Empress has ruminated over this since she first heard of it, the notion of people relying on materials other than what is won in the hunt to cover their nakedness. It is as if madness is spreading, and the out-worlders are the cause of the malady.

Empress Semiramis looks at this party of out-worlders and she sees they can't entirely be a poverty case. Their leading man, he obviously owns slaves, at least four that he has brought here with him to the royal court. Empress Semiramis looks at this tall, black skinned specimen of an other-worldly alien in his affectation of the local dress, and at the apparel of his slave girls. They must be slaves, for they wear leather harness upon their shoulders. Each one of them in her harness has a tool, a strange looking tool that the queen cannot discern the use of, yet it must be of some value to these slaves in their work, because the harness seems to *holster* the tool in such a way as to make it easy to take by the handle, and *draw*. These slave girls, or concubines, they must be slaves for look at them wearing the lowest form of dress: woven fabrics of what, linen or silks? Surely they are slaves.

Then Empress Semiramis begins to evaluate the oddity. This great alien who has clearly gone out of his way to mimic her people's proper dress, he has two other servants with him, an oddly appointed female, and a male of ridiculous comportment. If this leading, or chief man from another world has four slave girls he is able to keep in line, why is there also these other two? As the Queen evaluates the demeanor of the woman all the way to the back, it is clear that woman is not the bride or concubine of the chief man. Then what could she possibly be? She wears white, all white, now why would that be? Empress Semiramis has heard that females of other worlds typically, traditionally wear all white on the day of their nuptials. How odd, not feathers, or furs, or even the best leather or animal hides. The other worlders are so odd as Semiramis and her people reckon them and their ways. Semiramis has even heard of these women on other planets delighting in the wearing of white *silk* on their wedding days. She heard it said that this silk is something excreted by worms. Again: not something won by the hunter, taken in the kill, and then rendered by the work of the people of the village. Semiramis is beginning to find a very certain level of disgust in all people from other worlds. Just look at the other man in this present delegation of aliens. He wears what he surely considers to be fine *fabrics*, as if anyone other than the hopelessly indigent or insane could ever don *fabric* and be happy with it. The bizarre man actually wears black, mostly black. His shirt is white, and maybe he is a slave, because about his neck he appears to wear a collar of black fabric. It is all most disturbing, and that's not even taking into account the extremely strange aura he projects. Simply put, the queen feels as if this other man, a servant, is weird in numerous ways she may never even know. It must be why he is a servant, probably a slave, and has risen to no higher a station in this life. Why don't these people wear more feathers? That is the question that Semiramis finds of to be of such consternation. She takes a second look at the man who seems a slave, and yet couldn't be. He holds himself as if he is waiting for the moment when he must intervene. This man isn't just a slave, to Semiramis it is clear he is the Major Domo: he is the leading man amongst the slaves. The woman in white, she wants to be the leader amongst the slaves, and yet it is clear: the only time she is the leader, the decision maker, is when she is alone, on her own, or when she has only one other to contend with, someone she can manipulate. The woman in white reminds Semiramis of the type of servant that she sends out in the dark of night to kill troublemakers.

What makes these seven strangers interesting is how different they are from the one out worlder that Empress Semiramis knows best, the man who first called himself a missionary, and then got lost in realm of nubile and amorous native girls, the man who calls himself Father Drake. When he first arrived he spoke only of the mission he was on to share his faith with the people of this world, and yet something changed his priorities. To Semiramis he was a failure, and she was the one who made him so. Would these strangers prove to be similar? Probably not, they surely have a different purpose, and they are clearly unified in that cause. Father Drake was sent here alone, and Semiramis went out of her way to distract Drake from his mission work, she even went so far as doing herself the work of seducing the man. Too bad he proved to be sexually impotent. Oh well he did have a functional manhood, yet it became clear that his seed was of no fertile value in the womb of Semiramis, and thus he was of no value for her, not even as breeding stock. Beside that his skin was a pale abomination that when questioned about it, he used the words: 'white, Caucasian, and Caucasoid', although those words never made sense of what malady of birth had caused his skin to not be blue.

Semiramis has healthy, bright blue skin just as do most of the women of her court. Well, peasant women have dark blue skin and the deeper in poverty those women are, the darker their skin.

Many of the men in the court of Empress Semiramis are possessed of skin tones that vary. Most males have darker skin tones than females, and that befits their role as hunters. Father Drake was heard to describe the men's skin tone as *cobalt*, as if that word would ever make sense to Semiramis or her people. Thinking of Father Drake again causes the queen distraction, and she begins to recall what he was able to do with her in the bed chamber, in spite of his impotency. Father Drake never could have sown offspring into her womb, yet what he did for her, or rather *to her*, those were memories the queen would always carry. It lead to her working hard in effort find a replacement lover, and she had failed. Semiramis declared it legal for her to take for herself conjugal privileges with any man of the court, be he married or otherwise. Having gone through nearly all the men of her court she hadn't found a man so proficient at love play that he could be her replacement for Father Drake. No, the men of her court had only given her offspring, not actual sensual ecstasy. Semiramis considered making law that required men to give her sexual climax, or be punished. Despite her cravings, she knew it was a poor idea. You can ask only so much of men. Semiramis did make clear declarations that any act of sexual conquest initiated on her part was lawful, and could never be questioned under the law. The fact is that Semiramis needs lovers, indeed, a myriad of lovers. Her husband lost to her, she is without comfort, without consolation, and thus it is only a thing of charity for the women of her realm to share their husbands with her when she calls upon them to make their effort to satisfy their queen. That is the view Semiramis has taken since the death of

Emperor Ninus. From the very moment she stood over his dead body she resolved that nothing would ever again impede her carnal desires or obstruct her sensual appetites. At that time Semiramis signed the first edict making lawful her every act of lust. Standing over her husband's dead body, blood on her hands, she signed the edict, the inkwell of the quill pen filled with red from the pool at her feet. That night was bitter sweet for Semiramis, for while she had lost a husband, the most virile and vigorous man she'd ever known, never again would she have to bow to the demands or edicts of a man. From that moment on she was queen, and her rule has been absolute. Now she must display before these petitioning visitors that strength of will that makes her rule absolute.

"I am the Empress Semiramis, and you are in my court. Know that you can be judged and sentenced for any unlawful act or even any misspoken word here in my realm. I am Semiramis, queen over every tribes and every nation. I rule all here, and by your presence here you are also subject to my law, my whimsy, for I am queen. Kneel and grovel to show that you possess any little bit of understanding!" the queen tells her guests.

Yandi Yodel looks at Semiramis in clear surprise. He's never been confronted with such demands. While Yandi Yodel has dealt with a great many important persons in his life, he's never been greeted with such weighty demands. Then Yandi sees how the others now do as the queen demands. So Yandi begins by getting down on one knee. The others are already all the way down, their faces pressed to the floor. Yandi starts to put his other knee down when he hears the queen call for him to stop.

"Not you, not their chief man. You now stand, I give you leave. You have my permission," Semiramis calls out to Yandi.

He works hard to suppress a frown as he struggles to resume his feet. Once again standing, Yandi takes a moment to wait for a signal that it is his time to speak to the queen. For the moment she is just sitting there, apparently appraising him by eye.

"You wear dress that is traditional to your people?" the queen asks.

"I wear what I was told would be acceptable in the court of Empress Semiramis," Yandi replies. He can feel Excelentia now looking at him with all her animosity. She told him to play up the traditional dress story, as if these feathers and furs were his daily wear.

"I don't know what you want here, strange out-worlder. I already know you are impotent, speaking *sexually*. So what can you do for me?" asks the queen.

Yandi stands silent for more than a moment, more than two. He absolutely does not think of himself as *sexually impotent*. What sort of reasoning prompted this mad woman to say such a thing; especially to someone she'd just met, in the context of a formal meeting? He decides to speak to her directly about the issue that brought him here. "Empress, you have made bargains and pacts with a man you knew as Jasper Ignis. You traded with him for certain land rights, particular mineral rights. This agreement was wide ranging, and very encompassing. However you should know that

Jasper Ignis is now dead, and I come to you as his sole inheritor," Yandi explains.

"Jasper Ignis is dead? Woe to Jasper Ignis. He was a satisfying lover, and handsome in his own way, for an out-worlder of pasty, miss-colored complexion. Yet he was not a hunter, and his soul will languish in the dry, barren lands of the afterlife, until the final day when the last hunter has passed from this world, and finds his lodge waiting for him in the golden stalking grounds where true men, hunting men, can always find good game, and their brides wait in the lodge for their men, wait for the moment they can clean and cook the kill their man brings home. Jasper Ignis knew little to nothing about this life that we the good people, the blessed people, are given to live by our gracious gods, the gods of the hunt. Jasper Ignis is dead you say? Then any agreement I made with Jasper Ignis dies with him. You wish to speak of agreements? You desire to make a pact with Empress Semiramis? Then you must strike a fresh pact, and you will pay a more weighty price than did Jasper Ignis for what you desire. Jasper Ignis was a capable lover who pleased this Queen. I know not what pleasure you could bring this Queen in her bed chamber, and perhaps now I want to keep those odd rocks and dirt Jasper Ignis sought. Yet Jasper Ignis is dead. I have no record of what you say I agreed to with him, and I see nowhere any payment he made to me. So if I made agreement with Jasper Ignis, then that agreement is dead, and if you trouble this Queen too much, woe to you, for then you also will be dead!" thus declared Empress Semiramis.

Yandi takes a pause before he speaks his response. He takes onto his face the most subtle smile, and then Yandi speaks: "You are a blessed people, I see that now with my own eyes, where before I had heard it spoken only with my ears. Good Queen Semiramis, I do not suppose I could please you in your bed chamber, or would I even try. It is not my way, not the way of my people. My people are not like your people. You are a race of hunters, and my people rely little on the bounty of the hunt. The gods led you to the hunt, and the gods led my people to be traders. Just as did Jasper Ignis, I intend to establish a mining operation here on your world, and that I will be operating within the law I will compensate you, good Queen. All of this will be happening according to the agreement you made with Jasper Ignis, only now your agreement will be with me, and not him. Mineral ore is the wealth of my people just as the prey of the hunt is the wealth of your people. I expect you will comply with the agreement you made with my predecessor."

Even though everything Yandi Yodel said is technically true, a wave of anger, a visible rage, moves through the chamber, and the nexus of that rage is the Empress Semiramis herself. She is not the eye within the tempest, because the eye within a tempest is always calm. Semiramis is the burning hot core of the firestorm that waits to burst. By the reckoning of Semiramis this strange, oddly dressed, alien man dares to come to her world, her court, her throne room and speak of the terms she will be required to comply with, to yield? Semiramis has killed men for less presumption. Yet Semiramis does not explode, she does not burst with rage, rather the queen chooses to continue the exchange, although on a far less friendly footing. "You are a fat, overly tall, and mis-colored man. You should know that, just as you should know you are not the only petitioner before my court seeking the land rights you have mentioned. It seems mineral ore is the wealth of many people, and unless you are able to outbid the whole of the Bellazar Consortium, then I suggest you temper your tongue."

Silence follows. Yandi struggles, trying to think what could be said, what he could possibly do. He tries to recall what he saw Jasper Ignis do in the past. Yandi saw Jasper successfully plow his way through more than a few negotiations with a heavy hand. Yet at this very moment Yandi can't think at all how taking a heavy hand would advance his cause. Also he's struggling to overlook the insults Semiramis has tossed out with ease. The woman now shows herself outright to be a bigot. He won't be given any more time to think though. Semiramis wants to fire off another salvo.

"You and all your people, misshapen, ill colored of skin, and poorly proportioned. Has any member of your race ever successfully completed a hunt? If so, I can't imagine how. You are travelers, miners, and you barter. Your whole race is cursed by the gods it seems, because I see you here before me in ridiculous costume, attempting to buy from me from a position of poverty, not knowing your wealthy better has already out bid you. Look at yourself, Yandi Yodel, stupid, ugly, misshapen, poor, cursed by the gods, and oh yes: sexually impotent," Semiramis declares with a look of scorn come over her face, and then she tells the armed men of her court: "Kill them!"

****

It was an awful occurrence. The peace had held for so long, and then strangers had returned to Aborto Espontáneo Blanco. Naturally these strangers were antagonizing the established order of things. Father Drake had worked so hard to bring the people together, and teach them right from wrong. As a missionary he had managed to attract a following, and was vigorous in his efforts to disciple these few faithful adherents. Right now Father Drake watches one of his special congregants leave the cave he is forced to call home. He delights in the sight of her naked blue buttocks as the adolescent native girl walks out to collect fire wood to prepare the meal. Another of his disciples, she lay naked in his arms, and the darling was still asleep. Father Drake hoped to lie here in his cave, relaxing in full repose, until the meal was ready. Then his third disciple comes running into the cave, tragically she's wearing the few scraps of leather that are typical for the tribal girls of this odd planet when they move about going through their day to day chores. In spite of what teachings Father Drake has struggled to instill in his youthful congregation, he can't break them of every old habit. So while Father Drake yearns to live as the head of a commune composed of naked teenage girls, the members of his congregation at times still dress up in their typical native garb. 'You can't have it all,' Drake must so very often remind himself.

The native girl, her bright blue skin glistening with light perspiration, she comes running into the cave, jabbering in her native tongue too fast for Drake to follow. So he holds up one hand, and after a moment the girl takes pause for a deep breath, and then starts again, slower: "You told me watch for the sky, for falling from sky, and there is falling from sky."

Feeling nervous, Drake asks: "What is falling from the sky?"

"Like giant colorful stones, very round, very colorful, and all have covering floating overhead, following stones as they fall. Is very strange sight, I saw giant burning bird spit out bright round stones that now fall. Thought burning bird spit them out from the highest part of the sky. Surely bird is hiding in the dome of the sky now, hiding from wrath of gods," the girl explains.

"I need my shirt, the one with the special collar," Father Drake says, getting to his feet now, trying to move rapidly, without disturbing the girl that has been resting with her head on his breast. He also had to pull out of storage his black pants, and the simple belt he wore with the *clergy blouse*. Drake took a moment to see how dingy the tab collar might be, and was surprised how clean he found it. How long has it been since he's had to wear this thing? Last he remembered, Drake thought he was done with the clergy blouse and the tab collar. He'd absently told one of his girls to clean it, and put it into storage. Now one of his girls has dug it out from under a pile of things here in the cave. He doesn't know their names, the adolescent girls of his congregation; he just knows he has them completely convinced that doing whatever he wants is their key to paradise. Yet now he has to scramble to find, and divert the newly arrived strangers.

The strangers must be diverted, led about on foolish errands as much as possible. This is what Drake knows he must do before Semiramis learns about them, and before the Queen decides she is compelled to take a hand. When Drake isn't busy *pleasing* Semiramis, she allows him to do what he will, and that has meant establishing his collective commune of unmated females that see him as their spiritual guru, and ultimate arbiter of all their decisions, the every choice they make. In short, Father Drake has been leading all too comfortable a life filled with carnal indulgence. If he lets too many outsiders interfere, then it will all be over. Talk about a cause to make a man rush.

Father Drake was there when we made touch down. After we arrived in-system, and after we made planetary orbit, we deployed. Captain Malloy dropped his ship down into the atmosphere only as low as was necessary before having us thrown off his ship, thrown out into space. It was a seeming chaotic affair. We were rushed into modified drop-pods even as the deck apes were still rigging everything for our deployment. A large cargo hatch was dropped open about the same moment the chief of the boat came by my pod to shut, seal, and secure the whole thing. Then the inexplicable happens.

"Just in case I never get to see you again," the man says before he leans in to kiss me on the cheek. I nearly start to thrash my way out of the pod. I nearly start to scream at him demanding explanation, and nearly shouting recriminations. Yet I do none of that. I just lie there in the fetal position as the drop pod requires, and stare at him. I try to deny the part of me that says: *'you have wanted him to do that.'* I have a part of me that calls out: *'you must report him upon return to the ship.'* I don't know what part of my psyche compels it when I do speak, and the Chief of the Boat, he's closed the drop pod before I do utter a single word of response, yet when I do speak, I say: "We'll finish this when I get back."

What the heck did I mean by that? What was I saying? That idiot deck ape, he's gone and created a ton of confusion inside my head just at mission time. I'm going to kill him, after I skin him alive, and spit in his eye then I will surely kill him. Why is he always looking at me? Why does he always smile when he catches me looking his way? The man's behavior is entirely inexplicable, and I now begin to consider him intolerable. Oh God, I hope I'm not too much of a mess on my return, you know, when he will see me again.

Just as these thoughts conclude I feel the sealed drop pod begin to move. Moving, it begins to fall, and falling, the terror of free falling through space nearly causes me to scream like a mad woman. Then the pod deploys its parachute. This arrests the fall only slightly, and a jarring jerk hits me like the punch of a heavy weight slugger. I begin to pray for my own life. I think that's what I prayed for, because I can't be sure. If you recall I'm a Pentecostal, and the type of Pentecostal that prays in a tongue I can't necessarily interpret. Its complex, I know, and while I am sure some of you know what I'm getting at, most you don't. I'm off subject, so let's get back to it. I'm falling through space, or more accurately, I'm falling through the upper layers of the atmosphere of Aborto Espontáneo Blanco. I recall that's the odd, awful name they gave this planet. Soon I'll see the place is greener than any arboretum. For the moment all I know is I'm falling, it seems falling wildly through the air, dropping like a graceful, gliding stone.

I didn't really pay best attention to the mechanics of our deployment method. We aren't falling like stones, because the parachutes are good quality, self-guiding constructs. The deployment really began when Captain Malloy fired into the atmosphere a homing beacon that set down dead center at our desired drop zone. Our drop pods and parachutes actually steer us toward that beacon so subtly I don't even sense the changes in course and speed as they happen. Unlike our last drop, considered a covert insertion combat drop, this particular insertion isn't hidden at all. Major Octavia and Captain Malloy are not worried about who sees us, and we are even scheduled to have a local contact waiting to greet us. We fall, and we touch down all within fifty yards of the beacon. We are a lucky lot for that, I assure you. Immediately we scramble to get our weapons and gear into order. You might think we would want to hide our chutes and the drop pods, yet the local wildlife holds veto over such an obligation. Monkeys, rats, and so many other creatures attack the parachute silk as if it were the most valuable or most evil thing they've ever seen. They scream in frenzy tugging and striving to tear at our descent gear. I'm surprised we are not accosted ourselves, yet each one of us is armed. How the wild monkeys know that, I'll never guess.

Chapter Six

It was before he properly introduced himself that I saw Father Drake tossing out fruit from a sack he carried, fruit that the wild monkeys and rats went after with even more frenzy than they desired the parachute silk. My girl White was following him, and she was reaching into his bag to pull out and cast fruit just like Father Drake was doing.

"So what's this then?" I ask, addressing both the strange man, and my medic who seems to have attached herself to him.

"The monkeys will leave our stuff alone if we feed them," White tells me, cheer filling her voice.

"I hope you are a gracious bunch, because this stuff comes from my private supply, and it's the best way to buy off the gibbons," the strange man says with a smile.

"What's so special about it?" I demand as I go to take a piece of fruit for my own examination. "You've met then?" I ask, looking White dead straight in the eye.

"Father Drake found me first. So he helped me first, and now he's letting me help him to help us! He's a missionary, so you and Green will love him, I guess," White tells me as she tosses out a few more pieces of fruit. I notice neither Drake, nor White is eating any, yet I fail to take that as a hint.

I bite into the piece of fruit I procured, and instantly I know the poison. Also I curse myself for not sniffing at the fruit first, yet the pungent smell was mostly contained under the skin. "Your man Irwin had better stuff at his bar, and it didn't leave your hands and mouth messy with juice," I say through a terrible grimace. "The fruit has gone bad, in the way of homemade hooch," I conclude.

"Yeah, but without kettle, or copper tube, and all that stuff, what else am I going to do out here?" asks the man that White calls *Father Drake*. His smile is too inviting, and I'm not drawn in, not at all. Indeed, his smile actually makes me suspicious. "If you want the gibbons off of your things, and more importantly, if you want them off of you, then we have to give them something they will want more, and that's the fermented fruit," Drake tells me, as he is tossing the last of his natural liqueur candies to the wildlife.

"I suppose they can be a real danger?" I ask, even though it is Father Drake I'm giving all of my suspicion. Well, most of it. I might be warming up to the guy.

"These gibbons will mostly just harass you, with a strong possibility of stealing your smaller, easy to run off with things. The larger primates will perpetrate outright rape. At least the Beta Males do so," Father Drake informs, and his mere mention of such unpleasant possibility undoes whatever good will he was cultivating with me. Also, this is when I hear the click.

"It actually does him credit to provide such warning," I hear Green say as she makes approach. Her revolver is drawn, and she's pointing the weapon straight at Father Drake. Her rifle hangs from a sling, her other hand holding it still. "Yet I don't approve of his methods. Alcohol is a demon I've always despised," Green continues. When did she start to carry a revolver? It's like the things have come into vogue without my knowing.

"These are only our first moments here, Lieutenant. Perhaps we ought to be more pliable, even as it regards our pet peeves," I tell her, and instantly see the unspoken protest of her body language.

"Perhaps we should dispense with all notions of pleasantries, and bowing to this man's foibles," the unmistakable voice of the Major is calling out as she approaches, a patch of darkness emerging from the jungle. "We need to be about our mission, and to know me is to know I can stomach no delay," the Major goes on.

"Yes, Major," I reply, then I'm looking at Green and White, saying: "The beacon, we need to gather it, and all of the pods into the widest clearing these woods have to offer, and where is Tiger, she's got no excuse from the working party."

"Tiger has her sniper rifle aimed at our newest friend here, and I desire it stay that way for the present. Commander, you take the others and gather the beacon to the pods," the Major tells me. She's speaking to me, yet she is looking at Father Drake, her eyes actually locked on him as if she's intent to cut him down should he even flinch.

Once her soldier girls are away from the subject, Major Octavia begins to speak with him: "You will take us to the nearest village to speak with their chief."

"I can do that. I can do better. I can take you straight to the court of Queen Semiramis," Father Drake says.

"No, I want to talk to the nearest local, leading man," Major Octavia stresses to the man.

"Well, if you insist, we can do that, yet I think you should first go to the Anishinaabe rather than the Tsitsistas. It will just work out better that way, you can trust me on this," Father Drake says with a smile and wink of his eye.

"We will go to the closest village, and talk to their headman," the Major insists, even though she may have no means at all of discerning if this man is misguiding her and the soldier girls.

"Right then, once your troops have their chore done, I'll take up lead as your guide, and you will be in an audience with your headman in no time," Father Drake attempts to assure the Major.

"You will guide, you will not lead. I can't risk you on point, you are much too valuable an asset," Major Octavia tells him.

"Well it is good to be appreciated," Father Drake says with a smile.

Their conversation is interrupted by the sight and sounds of the soldier girls hauling their drop pods into the clearing. White and Green have their own, while Commander Black is pushing the Major's pod over the grass.

"Line them up nearby the beacon. Someone go help Tiger bring hers in. We have to get moving, and daylight is burning fast," the Major calls out.

I point White in the direction of Tiger's drop pod, I saw it just moments ago when I was fetching the Major's pod. While the girl runs to get Tiger and her pod, Green and I work to place the pods in a formation the Major outlines for us.

"Circle them around the beacon. No, leave a gap, about twenty feet should do. Not there, along the magnetic north, yeah, that's it," the Major is barking at us as we work. Then White is returning, dragging Tiger's pod as Tiger is weighed down with her sniper rifle. Her weapon system is heavy as every single piece, every little bit is metal. Not one piece is plastic, not any little bit is carbon fiber. No, this time out our sharp shooter is going old fashion, heavy duty weapon system. Goodness, with the weight of her weapon and ammunition, I could carry ten of my scout carbines and a hundred rounds of ammunition for each rifle, and still be under the weight Tiger carries. Well, maybe I exaggerate, just a little. Just as we think we are done with the pods the Major comes over and she begins a sort of inspection I never anticipated. Also, she makes a gesture toward White and Tiger. The two girls figure it out before I do, and suddenly they are over with Father Drake talking up a storm as they turn him around so his back is to the pods. The Major checks each pod in turn. She visually examines some gear I never really noticed right up until this point. Really, I must be asleep on my feet not to have noticed that stuff. It's a series of high tension straps and some kind of collapsed bladder. It's all one rig, and there is an identical rig in each pod with one exception. In the Major's pod there is a ring piece that I didn't see in any other pod, and the ring has all sorts of clasps and buckles hanging from it. I'm not sure what all this is for, and as you have seen the Major doesn't clue us in on anything until her hand is forced.

With her inspection complete the Major looks at Green and me, saying: "Right, secure and seal them all, check and double check, then we are on our way."

So I get to work on half the chore, with Green doing the other half. Of course while we work the Major walks off to do something very interesting. In the blink of an eye she's gotten that fellow Father

Drake to turn around facing her, and she's got a knife waiting to wave in front of his face when he does turn. She says: "Now, the Tsitsistas are closer, so that's where we are headed, and if you do anything that slows us down, or impedes our course, I will cut you to pieces and feed you to the gibbons because we all know steak tartar is good for hangovers."

"You suggest I'm inclined to act in bad faith, why ever would you think so?" asks Father Drake.

"Because while you represent yourself as a priest, I can smell the sex on you from ten yards away, and while I have no idea what strictures your sect imposes regarding celibacy, I'm sure they don't want you going about with the scent of your carnal escapades wafting off you all through the day. Now, lead us to the Tsitsistas or I start cutting," Major Octavia says.

We march for the next hour. I'm at point with my scout carbine held ready. I have a .45 caliber long slide semi-auto pistol as my side arm. The thing is beautiful with its heavy carriage. Major Octavia is at the center of the marching line with the priest walking before her, and White behind. Tiger is at the lead, and Green maintains a position between me and Drake. The trail takes us down out of the higher hilly country to a plateau where we find a semi-permanent habitation. We walk in slowly, not wanting to be perceived as a threat. I watch Father Drake introduce the Major to the apparent Chief, and then the Major excludes the priest from her conversation with the chief. They talk about just what we came here to talk about: mineral rights, and how those rights are leased or sold here about. These people seem to be absolute primitives, because they have little to no idea about the value of mineral rights, or the exploitation of other natural resources at all. I'm no expert on the subject either, yet I at least have some idea about the concept. The Major also asks about how outsiders are viewed. She speaks very frankly to the Chief, never is she condescending, never does she talk down to him. It's amazing how bold she is with the man. I found the talk was boring. It was the reaction of the villagers to the presence of strangers that was interesting.

Father Drake was not of interest to them. They knew him, had apparently already taken their measure of him, and only the chief gave him any time. The rest, his people, they were neutral, or possibly even quietly hostile toward the man. Something about this guy, I'm telling you, he might just be bad business. Yet it could just be his missionary nature, some folks don't take kindly to that. No, the odd, interesting, and lively aspect of our visit was how the villagers reacted to us soldier girls. The adult males stood off, giving us hard stares. The adult females seemed to want to pretend we didn't exist, while all the youngsters were behaving as if we were a troupe of sideshow oddities from a traveling carnival. Seriously, the boys were standing much closer than were their adult male counterparts and the girls slowly yet surely began to walk right up to us. One tinny little girl was actually clinging to White by the bottom of her pant leg before anyone, even White, was even aware. They were fascinated by Tiger; it seems they had never before seen a ginger. The fact that her red hair hangs in long curly locks entirely lose was especially alien to them. Also, we were women wearing clothes: shirts *and* pants. These alien creatures wore animal hides, and only scant bits of it as necessary to cover their rude, naughty bits. It was a mind bending experience, these aliens with azure skin, dark braided hair, and actually aristocratic features. I swear, if not for the blue skin, and the almost complete nudity, Morganti would feel like she was surrounded by family.

"Are you sexually impotent?" I hear a voice ask.

Startled, I look about and realize a moment later the question was addressed to me by an adolescent girl standing just before me. "What kind of question is that?" I blurt out, without thinking.

"All of the out worlders we have ever seen, ever heard of, none of them can make children. Where do you all come from if you are all barren?" the girl asks.

"People make babies all the time. What are you on about?" I demand, looking at the girl as if she is crazed, and suspicion written on my face.

"Father Drake has lain with many of us females, and not one has born him any young. If he was to lie with you, would you bare young?" the girl asks.

I stand there stunned. I have no idea how to compose my response. Surely I am contending with native naiveté. My gut reaction is to spout some awful denial. Yet the larger truth is that I cannot reproduce. Not I or any of the other soldier girls are capable to conceive. We weren't built with that in mind. I'm about to try and make some reasoned, and softly spoken explanation when the Major begins to call out to us.

"We are marching again in two minutes people, two minutes and we are marching again!" shouts Major Octavia, and I notice the Chief of the

Tsitsistas is at her side, closer than Father Drake. People are bringing the Chief things, a satchel, a spear, and he puts on some heavy duty sandals.

I approach the Major and ask: "Is he coming with us?" I try to indicate the Chief of the Tsitsistas without anyone knowing I'm pointing to the guy.

"Yes, he wants to introduce us to his fellow Chief, the leader of the Anishinaabe," the Major tells me.

Shaking my head, just a little, I ask: "Do these names mean anything that we know of? Tsitsistas? Anishinaabe?"

"Of course they do, Commander. Tsitsistas simply means *the people*, while Anishinaabe means *original people*. Such translations are really quite common when dealing with indigenous peoples. Haven't you ever seen this? You were a frontier border patrol officer before we met, were you not?" asks the Major.

"Actually the indigenous tribal peoples we encountered were entirely hostile, so much so we usually only fought with them, never actually getting to talk," I respond.

"Never talked with the native? Not ever?" she asks.

"They were entirely allied with the local pirate and bandit gangs, so they only saw us as prey. We were their enemy before a word was ever spoken," I explain.

"Tragic, isn't it, how our work so often blocks us off from experiencing local culture," the Major says, looking off into the sky wistfully.

'She cannot be serious about that,' I'm left thinking.

Then the Chief of the Tsitsistas seems to indicate he is ready to go, and we begin to march out with the Chief, telling us what path to follow. Not Father Drake, he seems to have lost his place in the heart of our dear Major. Drake is left to follow after Major Octavia and the Chief, the two of whom seem to have taken up a fresh and invigorating friendship. Or perhaps the Major is just playing the man, leading him in the way she desires. I don't know, for I am one who has experienced difficulty leading the thirsty to water. With only an hour left of the light of day we reach the primary village of the Anishinaabe, and their reaction to us is only slightly easier to deal with than that of the Tsitsistas. I come to believe it must be our emissary, for this time the Chief of the Tsitsistas is our liaison, and Father Drake is relegated to affirming what is said by the Tsitsistas Chief, when he's asked, and as time passes Father Drake becomes more of a fixture on the scene than a participant.

As a casual afterthought the Major informs me we will be spending the night here. I haven't a moment to consider the logistics of this when I hear a bull scream. The sound is horrible, and my eyes bulge. White loses all color from her face and it actually seems out of place when Tiger whimsically says to us: "You have to kill it to grill it."

I don't say anything, yet I want to demand explanation from Tiger. The explanation comes from my executive officer, Lieutenant Green.

"They have guests, and they want to celebrate. Seven extra mouths to feed means at least seven more plates to serve up. What's wrong, Commander? Weren't you paying attention?" Green asks.

Actually I was paying attention. The only thing that didn't have my attention was the possibility that livestock was about to be slaughtered. I was watching how the Anishinaabe girls were so fascinated with Tiger. Unlike the Tsitsistas women, who were fascinated with Tiger's hair and good looks, these women are bewildered, and fascinated by the notion that Tiger is a *woman and a hunter*. It seems that gender roles among the Anishinaabe are far more strictly maintained than it was among the Tsitsistas. *Vive la difference!* There are other critical differences I take notice of as well. I was observing how close an eye my girl Green kept on Father Drake. While the man was becoming more and more *less* important to the process we were pursuing, endearing ourselves to the locals, Green was watching him like an eagle, or an owl. Ever had one of those things lock his eyes on you? When Green wasn't directly observing Father Drake, she was actually, *openly*, asking the locals about him, and it seemed she was getting the answers she wanted, or at least answers that satisfied her. The woman has no subtlety about her investigation either, pointing her finger right at the man as she questions local women and men about his habits, practices, and history with them. It makes me take a closer look at Father Drake, and I notice that he is not entirely alone here. While the Tsitsistas seemed to be avoiding him, or treating him with a certain disdain, I see young females at this village approaching him with unmistakable familiarity. Then I realize these are not girls of the Anishinaabe. While they are aliens to me with their blue skin, their flesh only scantily covered in reptile or animal hide, beyond that there is only subtle differences to be seen. The girls I see in the company of Father Drake, they bind or braid their hair differently. They tie and knot their breechclout different. Most of all, they wear feathers where none of the other women I've seen so far wear feathers. And the reaction they get specifically to their display of feathers is hard not to notice. These girls are setting themselves apart, and they don't seem to care that they do so. Actually as I take a close look at them I see that they are *very familiar* with Father Drake, and he actually seems to be forced by the girls to hold them to a distance for the sake of decorum. Also, while these girls exhibit practices that set them apart from any of the Tsitsistas or the Anishinaabe, they seem to be doing things that set them apart from each other. I know that seems to be a big step, a far leap in deductive reasoning. Some might say *'don't read too much into any one thing'* yet I think I'm making a sound observation. The girls who come and go from the presence of Father Drake, each one of them seems to be from a tribe or clan different from all her fellows. I know; I base that simply on how they tie the thongs they wear or how they affix the feathers in their hair, yet the totality of small subtle details, when all brought together, makes for an unbreakable argument. Father Drake has done something here, especially with these particular girls that makes the missionary he is supposed to be abhorrent to the people he's been sent to as a messenger. Father Drake has defeated his purpose here on this world by some aspect of his conduct.

I try to turn my attention back to what's important, the talks about mining rights, and how the tribal chiefs feel about the issue. I'm seeing how the Major wants to know how these men feel about the dispensation of their land's natural wealth before she goes to Empress Semiramis to present her case for the mineral rights. I'm trying to better observe how the Major works with these alien men on this difficult, complex issue, and yet I'm distracted.

"They won't leave me alone now, and I paid them to go away," White is practically crying to me as she walks my way with two small children clinging to her legs, actually riding along as she takes her strides.

"What are you even talking about?" I ask as I see the children affixed to the unit medic.

"They were so cute, and I gave them candy, but that made them ask for more, so I gave them more candy, and they wanted more, but I needed them to leave me alone, so I told them I would give them more candy if they left me alone, and they took that candy, but then they said I had to give them more candy, and I'm running about of candy, and I don't know what to do," White says.

"Good God, girl, they are aliens, physiology we have no knowledge of, you may have been feeding them poison enough to kill them," I tell the girl in sharp tone.

"I don't think so. They told me they were hungry and needed the candy or they would die," White says in response.

"*They told you?* You allowed children to convince you how much *candy* they may or may not need? These are primitives, White, they are as conniving as any other children you may ever encounter, and yet they are primitives, and may never before have had refined sugars. What you may have given them may be more dangerous than any narcotic or poison, combined. You are the unit medic, and here I find you in disregard of basic nutrition and xenomorph contact protocol?" I ask of the girl, and I then worry I've been too harsh.

"*Xenomorph?* That was a long time ago, and we aren't even in that service anymore, Commander," she says, and instantly I go from being worried I was too harsh to wanting to slap her for impertinence.

"Don't back talk me, you little idiot, you are the one with two space aliens affixed to you. What's going to happen if their over protective mother sees you possibly abducting her offspring? Did you think about that?" I demand. My tone with her now as harsh as it's ever been without raising my voice.

Then for a moment I think it fortunate when we are rescued from further consternation or confrontation when two of the adult females come to gather up the youngsters, yet these females become full of protest. One takes up a child, pulling it off the leg of my girl white, and she clearly wears a look of scorn as she turns away, clutching the youngster to her breast. The second takes up her child, and then looks at me hard, saying: "I don't want your strange daughter feeding my children any more of your poison food."

I turn a hard eye on White, and make no mistake I am reprimanding her with this harshest glare I can manifest. This is full eye contact, a Commander not pulling any punches. We can't have some silly indiscretion, or slight misjudgment derail all the work the Major is accomplishing in these talks with the tribal chiefs. Then I see the girl's lips start to quiver, and I feel crushed. I grab a hold of her, and put my arm around her shoulders. "Oh God, my dearest, I'm sorry, we just have to be so careful, and tread lightly, yeah?" I say to her.

The alien mother is still there, still giving us her own hard look, and she says: "You nearly denied this one being your daughter, and it would have been such a lie." Then she's turning away, walking off with her child in arms without giving me my chance at rebuttal. Of course the babe in her arms is holding out its hand in hopes for more candy as the mother takes it away.

"Don't ever leave me," I hear myself mutter without being aware I was expressing any such sentiment. I don't know where those words come from, or why I said them, I just know at the moment I was squeezing the girl's shoulders even harder than before.

The next several days went on just as the first. We went to a village. The Major held talks with the Chief and depending on how she did at the previous village, the previous Chiefs would be there, either supporting her, or decrying her proposals. As I told you, we went from the Tsitsistas to the Anishinaabe, and then venturing out even wider, we went to the Beothuk, a tribe so family oriented that their name literally translated as *Kinfolk*. They were indeed close relatives of the Anishinaabe. In a lighter moment, I suggested their name meant *Bee Thumpers*, yet no one seemed to understand my reference. They even began to look about for any hives the Beothuk may have maintained, and found none. I could only shake my head in disappointment. Later, some of the women folk of the Beothuk asked me to sample their cakes. When I distinctly tasted honey I tried to share this with my comrades. Yet when I attempted to introduce the honey cake making women to my soldier girls, none of those women could be found. I found myself humiliated twice in one day, it was bad, and yet nowhere near my record. Anyway, we went on to the next village.

From the Beothuk we went to the Degexit'an (*People of this land*), from the Degexit'an we went to the Dena'ina (*The People*). Word was spreading, and the Major's success was leading not only to a propensity for Chieftains to be predisposed to agree with whatever she proposed, it actually became a rather warped process. The notion that one tribe had fed the Major their best foods meant the next tribe felt compelled to make an effort to feed her *their better foods*. Grilled beef, fire roasted pork, oven baked poultry, and yes, *honey cakes* were being thrust at us as if entire groups of people's self-esteem depended on how compulsively we gorged ourselves on the feasts we found ourselves being presented with. I think we were at a joint gathering of the Dene (*The People*) and the Dene Tha (*The True People*) that I, absent of mind, complained about the way we were being expected to eat.

"Haven't you ever run for public office?" the Major asks of me, with a sly grin upon her face.

From the *Dene* and *Dene Tha* combine we go on to visit two more tribes, The *Dine'e*, and the *Dunne-Za*, (respectively *The People*, and *The Real People*), and according to the Major the results she has managed gain are just grand. Of nine tribes visited, seven agreed enthusiastically with all she worked to convince them, and three of the Chiefs have agreed to guide us to the court of Empress Semiramis and stand at the Major's side when she presented her proposal to the queen. For a moment the Major thought of having papers of *Proxy Support* drawn up, and yet we quickly recalled there is little to no written language among the various people we have visited. The papers would have proven the support of the seven of the nine chiefs. As it is, the Major will have to rely on the eye-witness testimony of the three chiefs we will have at our side.

"Do you know what rubbish eye-witness testimony is?" the Major asks me, clearly exasperated.

"Well, isn't it considered the most reliable form of testimony?" I ask, because I'm an idiot who doesn't know to just agree and move along. Perhaps I'm too comfortable, sitting as I am against a wooden support post in a hut in the village of the *Dunne-Za*.

"I should tell you about just a few of the occasions where I've manipulated people's testimony, literally molded it, re-shaped it into something almost completely the opposite of what it was when I first heard it. It's almost like most people have minds of mush," the Major responds.

"You never did that with me, did you?" I ask, suddenly feeling unsettled.

She turns to me, pulling off her dark glasses so very suddenly, and the Major is looking into my eyes as she tells me: "No! I would never try anything like that with you!" Then the Major takes hold of me by the face, setting her hands on either of my cheeks, and she goes on: "Oh! What makes you think such a thing? Don't you know how special you are to me? I would never! Please tell me you understand? Please tell me you trust everything I say?"

I sit there, silently mouthing the work *'yes'*, this weird moment stretching out until the Major bounces my head against the wooden post I've been leaning my back against.

"And to think, I only put a quarter of my possible manipulative skill into that one effort," the Major says as she's standing up and putting her dark glasses back on before she walks away.

Among other things I will take away from this moment is my new knowledge of what sturdy structural framing the Dunne-Za are capable of, I mean really, the support post and the Major have taken me to the precipice of a concussion.

So we set out bright and early the very next day, headed for the capitol, or at least the closest thing to a capitol on this very primitive planet. Seriously, it's like we've been visiting the Madagascar of Queen Ranavalona the First. Well, I haven't seen anything as bad as that yet, not here. Hopefully I never will, and I do understand I just jinxed myself, and all the people I love.

We march for the capitol an entire day, and have to camp out for the night. We marched with the three Chiefs, one of them from the Tsitsistas, who has been with us from the beginning, and the other two from the Dena'ina and the Dine'e. The Chiefs, even though they were considered to have VIP status by the Major, were very helpful to us both marching, and when we had to make camp. It makes sense though, considering this is their home territory as they have been living here all of their lives. They are excited to a part of a trip to the capitol. Yet it turns out two of the Chiefs have other agendas. This came to light when the Chief of the Tsitsistas told Major Octavia he was willing to allow her to marry him. He said one of his half-dozen brides had recently passed away from old age after thirty years, and so he had room in his hut for one more wife.

"You were married to her for thirty years?" asked the Major.

"No, she was thirty years old when she died, typically the end of a woman's beauty, you understand," the Chief replies, nodding his head knowingly.

About the same time as the Tsitsistas Chief proposed to marry our Major, the Dine'e Chief took a big hold of White by the girl's bottom and told her "I like candy also..." Really, that's what he said to her. The Dine'e Chief must have heard what had happened with the children at the Anishinaabe village, or was it the Tsitsistas village? It's been a busy week, and we still have ground to cover before we are before the throne of the Queen to make our case for the local mineral rights.

Just so no one forgets, let me remind you that Father Drake is still in our company. He's been so quiet that I've forgotten what his voice sounds like, yet we are still inundated with his presence. He's watching everything we do, and even though the Major and the Chiefs have no need for him at their conferences, he still sits right there, as if there were a placard with his name carved on it placed before his chair. The only thing that distracts Father Drake from keeping tabs on everything the Major and the Chiefs talk about are those adolescent girls who step out of the jungle like shadows, and fade back in like ghosts. At least three times a day, and a few more times at night it seems those young girls are calling on him as if *he* is the highest priority in their lives. I can tell you this stuff about Father Drake because Lieutenant Green is telling me. In angry, hushed voice she tells me after pulling me aside at least once a day, and then remind me what sort of activities Father Drake is up to, as if he and what he does is a mission priority. What is it about the guy that has her so fired up, and cross about him? I suppose I should ask at some time. I'll get around to it before it's too late, I'm sure.

Chapter Seven

Spears fall level with the floor, and the tip of every spear is pointed at the bellies of the court visitors. Queen Semiramis is laughing at them, laughing at her visitors as if they are pets she is allowed to kill on a whim.

"Bellazar knows you are here. They have a means of contacting me, and I confirmed what they asked after. They seem to already know outsiders are here on my world trying to undermine the good faith agreement I have made with them, and Bellazar will be here soon to contend with those who work against their interests. I will have no compunction about giving you over to them. The only question being will I do so with you still alive, or dead?" states Queen Semiramis.

Xavier's Seraphim have made their own decision about the notion of being taken, alive or dead. They draw their weapons, and each begins to discharge rounds at the nearest of spear men. Gomer Mosley is billowing for Excelentia to remove Yandi from the area. She doesn't need the prompt. Excelentia is already rushing to grab hold of Yandi. She shouts: "We have to go, now!" as she pulls him toward the exit.

The only problem with leaving is someone has shut the doors. *'Did these people think wicker could hold me?'* Yandi wonders as he begins to run for the exit. Excelentia follows, and she is right behind Yandi as he smashes through the wicker portal. Then Excelentia is shocked as she sees a whole new visitor's delegation right there on the other side.

The soldier girls were in the act of raising their guns from the moment they heard a commotion from the other side of the sealed wicker doors. Then Yandi Yodel came bursting through. He tackles Commander Black spear fashion, drilling her good. Not with an actual spear, rather Yandi put his head down to stick the woman with a smashing tackle. Commander Black cries out, the blow not easy to take. Yandi Yodel drives on and smashes through another wicker divider, and only then does he give a slight lift before he drives downward, smashing Commander Black into the floor. Again she cries out, the pain difficult to endure.

This is when Lieutenant Green makes her move. Screaming: "Traitor!" as she slams the butt of her gun into the face of Father Drake, hitting him right between the eyes, knocking the man over. Then Green is on top of him, her submachine gun pushed aside so that she can smash his face with her fists and elbows. Green batters the man nearly to unconsciousness, and then she leans back. Speaking, Green says: "You told our enemies we were here, and you did it using those girls whose innocence you have stolen! Not a one of them is even twenty years old and yet you have made each of them your whore!"

"Don't you know how much little girls will do to please a man they think is god?" Father Drake asks, his voice emitting from his ruined face.

Green, driven to further rage by his comment, begins to pound on his face once again.

In the midst of so much chaos, the Empress Semiramis looks on, observing all that happens in her court. She watches her warriors die as they fought the out worlders. She watched the out worlders fall as their terrible boom weapons failed to bring down every warrior. The boom sticks are powerful, yet they lack a certain nuance, an alacrity that spears have as they can be thrust at bellies. Valeria Hogan went down first. Her sister Pricilla Hogan screamed, and turned her pistol on the warrior who killed Valeria. Then Pricilla fell to the warrior who was closest to her and had only hesitated while she had a gun trained on him. Tanya Petite suffered a deep cut upon her flank, and she made the decision to fall, playing dead. The warrior who had cut her, he should have double checked, yet he wanted to claim a kill this day. Nelly Silver suffered a spear stabbed into her face, and through her brain. It would be hard for Xavier Gosling to repair such damage. Empress Semiramis watched all this until some other sight captivated her eye. Another woman, and she was one of the out worlders, she was standing just outside the throne room. The moment Semiramis caught sight of this woman the Queen knew she had found another hunter.

Tiger heard a scream to both curdle and freeze her blood amidst all the chaos, and when she turned to look, Tiger saw one of the indigenous women coming her way. The alien woman drew a knife as she cast aside a massive and massively elaborate feather headdress. "What's going on?" Tiger asks, and then she is throwing up her rifle to block the slashing attack Queen Semiramis utilizes to initiate their duel. The Queen's warriors use their spears to clear the area for the duel. They knock aside the people standing nearby or they begin to hammer at those who are prone in their effort to make clear space for their Queen. "You are a hunter!" shouts Queen Semiramis, pointing the tip of her knife at Tiger.

"I'm a sniper, and yeah, I hunt," responds Tiger, her face a mask of confusion.

"To kill a hunter found among the out worlders will bring my people to their knees! When they learn I have killed a hunter among the out worlders they will shake with awe of their Queen!" Semiramis tells Tiger with lunatic exuberance.

"What is wrong with you?" shouts Tiger, and then she's forced to once again protect herself from the attack of Empress Semiramis. The Queen slashes at Tiger again, and then she has hold of Tiger's rifle barrel. The Queen makes a kind of rowing motion and pushes the rifle barrel downward, almost to the floor. She takes Tiger's balance, and for good measure Queen Semiramis gives Tiger a bump. Tiger falls over, rolling, and she draws her own knife as she regains her feet. Pointing the knife at Semiramis, Tiger says: "You want to fight? Then I will give you a fight."

"Re-match!" Gomer Mosley shouts as he dashes toward Major Octavia. He has a wild look in his eye, and he's extended his arms as if he plans to grab her by the throat to choke her lifeless.

With a circular motion of her arms and a slight side-step, Major Octavia has Gomer running past her, and tripping over his own feet to fall wildly. Also Octavia uses a punch dagger to give Gomer two quick stab wounds in the kidney area. Even though Gomer has fallen flat on his face, Octavia still takes three cautionary steps backward away from him. Then Octavia watches Gomer lift his legs backward, curling them around until he's set his feet down on either side of his head. She watches him shuffle his feet, going around in a circle clockwise until toes are pointed her way. Gomer begins to uncurl, lifting himself up until he's standing upright, and grinning at Octavia, he says: "You should know by now my kidneys aren't there anymore."

"Just force of habit, and I did stab something, didn't I?" asks Octavia.

"Damn it, just kill her!" shouts Excelentia as she comes storming in after Yandi. Excelentia is drawing her pistol and she begins to aim it straight at Commander Black. Excelentia wants to kill the other woman with a headshot. Then a screaming banshee leaps upon Excelentia, tackling her to the floor in swift motion. It is White that is upon Excelentia, bashing her in the face, and screaming a horrifying war cry every moment of her assault.

Yandi and Commander Black pause in their battle only for a moment, then Yandi says: "Good, we won't be interrupted again, not for some time at least." Then Yandi suddenly smashes Commander Black in the face with one of his beefy fists. Her skull is dense, very dense, and the punch hurts him almost as much as it has hurt her. Yet Commander Black is not beyond fighting back, and she captures the arm that he uses to abuse her. Commander Black begins to turn her body, attempting an arm lock. Yandi tries to pull his captured arm free while hammering blows against her face with his off hand. It becomes a brief interlude of herky-jerky motion. Commander Black is going to look puffy around the eyes in the morning, yet she's turned her body, and begins to apply pressure to his elbow joint. Yandi Yodel screams with anger of a sudden, and then he's lifting Commander Black up, only to slam her down with enough force to leave her feeling stunned, at least for a few moments. When Yandi begins to pull his arm free of her grip, Commander Black manages the quick transition: wrapping legs around his neck and shoulder in a *triangle choke*. Yandi begins throwing punches with his free arm, hitting her face hard. The man has a long reach and powerful fists. It is only because of his long reach that he's able to strike at her this way. He's also trying to raise himself again to deliver another big slam. Commander Black counters with a grab at his legs, hooking a hand behind his knee, and then a swing of her own legs that cause Yandi to fall. Yet he doesn't fall hard and when Commander Black rolls on top of him, Yandi easily throws her off. The man is strong, and he moves quickly. She may have brought him down, but all of this tussle cost her hold on him. He scrambles to get at her again, and Commander Black must protect herself. Yet she sees an opening and before he realizes, Yandi Yodel finds that Commander Black has wrapped her arms around his neck and shoulder in a choke that is almost identical to the one he'd escaped just moments before. He would scream his frustration if the world were not going so dark around him.

"I want to hear you say it!" shouts Lieutenant Green when she takes a pause from battering the priest.

Wracked with pain or feeling mostly numb, Father Drake lies there until he tries to speak. A weak spray of blood is all he is able to produce, sputtering red mess that becomes a stain around his mouth.

"I want to hear you say you aren't a real priest!" demands Lieutenant Green.

"I was when I first came here," says Father Drake, and then he is struggling to clear his airway of spittle made thick with blood.

"You are a monster! You pretend to be some kind of missionary when really you are something devious!" says Lieutenant Green, spitting her words in disgust.

"The retirement package for what I do now is so much better. I loaf most of the day, and have sex most of the night with nubile, adolescent native girls. When people actually come to this world I pretend to be a mediator between the out worlders and the natives, when really I'm an informer serving Bellazar. The native girls don't just service me sexually. I've taught those three I got right now to operate the communication transceiver given to me by Bellazar. You would not believe how responsive they are, and I'm sure they are headed here now with the express purpose to kill you all," Father Drake explains.

"And what are you going to do?" Lieutenant Green asks.

"I'll have my girls clean me up, and bandage me. Then I will again make full use of them, *sexually*," Father Drake says, smiling. Then he is chuckling.

This is when Lieutenant Green begins to hit the man once more. She takes the butt of her submachine gun and uses it to slowly, and methodically bash his skull until the bones are so broke his face caves in.

Queen Semiramis lets go of the rifle as she screams and is darting in to knife attack Tiger. The sniper turns away in a counter clockwise direction, and stabs the Queen in the Queen's shoulder. Queen Semiramis screams with lunatic fury, her body shaking from pain, and her mind rejecting the possibility that she's been handled so easily by an out worlder. Semiramis tries to turn toward Tiger in an attempt to retaliate, and finds she can't. The motion necessary to turn would aggravate her wound, possibly even tearing a blood vessel or cutting a major nerve. Queen Semiramis feels helpless, and suffers another terrible shock of pain when Tiger pulls free her knife.

Queen Semiramis instantly begins to fall to the floor, her face twisted with the pain she suffers. The Queen's guards instantly turn their spears on Tiger, and the Captain of the Guard says: "We'll give you one chance to leave."

Tiger quickly puts away her knife. They let her take up her rifle, and then Tiger backs away.

"You only ah... You just seem to have the one knife this time?" asks Gomer Mosley, his face covered with his bizarre and nauseating smile.

"You don't want a hum-drum repeat of our last encounter, do you?" Octavia asks of him, showing off a big smile of her own.

"You mean when that, I mean your redhead knocked me over, or when you, when in that terrible moment you stabbed me in the throat?" asks Gomer, his voice sounding like churning gravel.

"Stabbing you in the throat was fair play, and when last we met I should have dealt with you much more harshly for the way you dealt with my employee," Octavia explains, and the smile has faded from her face.

"I was ah... I say it was downright kind of me the way I dealt with your girl, after the way she hit me with that chair," Gomer insists, sounding agitated.

"I meant the employee you tortured, murdered, and nailed to a bathroom wall," Octavia responds, her face becoming a mask of hate.

"That was just a message between friends... Now don't be holding it against me. You know how to be professional. How's that old expression go? It wasn't personal, it was business..." Gomer tries to convince her, and before he can finish the thought, before he can say more, Major Octavia has drawn a large caliber, semi-automatic pistol and shot him in the chest three times.

"I really should have asked Commander Black before I borrowed her side-arm," Major Octavia says as she walks away from the falling body of Gomer Mosley.

Her opponent barely seems to notice when a long knife is shoved deep into the abdomen. How is that even possible?

Excelentia is nothing if not cool under pressure. Realizing someone has managed to get the drop on her; even knocking her over, Excelentia got a hold of her knife and stabbed it hilt deep into the belly of her attacker. The blade goes in just between the muscles of the abdomen, and because of the lack of reaction, Excelentia thinks she might need to twist the blade in the wound.

"You don't really know what I am, do you?" White asks the woman.

"I don't need to, I just need to get you off of me," Excelentia says with frustration as she twists the blade.

"I'm not human. I'm a Soldier Girl, and you? You are about to become the victim of a cliché," White says in a tense voice as she draws one of her snub nose revolvers and pushes the barrel hard against the face of Excelentia. In a quick series of motions White cocks the hammer and squeezes the trigger. The gun discharges and the limbs of Excelentia spasm, shake, and then fall limp. The woman is still, motionless, as White stands up off of her.

The awful man suddenly rolls, making her hold loose. Then he tries to use pure brawn to push her arms off. Except Commander Black has already reset her choke hold, and Yandi Yodel only has the one arm to push with. Perhaps if he'd pushed in rather than try to push off. Or if he'd driven in with and elbow and steady pressure he might have escaped, only Yandi Yodel had tried to muscle his way through, and it failed him.

When Commander Black stands up she finds White addressing a question to her: "He's dead? Did you have to kill him?"

"This is the second time he's beaten me black and blue. The Major is never going to forgive me for being so forgiving of him. The problem is I never get to fight with someone so proficient as well as so strong, that's what made me hesitant," Commander Black explains.

✳✳✳✳

I'm standing over a dead man. I didn't actually have to kill him, yet it is just as I said: this is the second time I've let this man give me a beating, and my boss isn't going to be happy about it. I look at my medic, and ask the obvious question: "How's that knife in your gut?"

"Well she stabbed me," White says, suddenly looking at the dagger protruding from her abdominal wound.

"Your acting like you don't even know you've been stuck in the gut," I say, sounding a little excited. I mean, she's got *a knife in her belly*.

"Well I turned off my pain receptors, I know how to do that," White tells me.

"You know how to do that? Why don't I know how to do that?" I ask.

"I'm the unit medic," she says, as if that's all there is to it.

"I'm the back-up medic, shouldn't I know?" I demand.

"You are the command node, and you hardly ever pay any mind to all the stuff you are supposed to know as back-up anything. You are the back-up sniper and these days I'd wager you'd have trouble hitting a target at three hundred meters," White tells me.

"Three hundred meters? You don't think I could hit three hundred meters?" I ask, clearly I have become indignant.

"Umm... Maybe I should rephrase the statement," White mutters, suddenly looking away.

"Maybe we should find the others. Did we set a rally point? I've forgotten what we were doing here in the first place," I say, sounding as if my patience is wearing thin.

"We were going to seek an audience with Queen Semiramis, until the brawl broke out, and I'm guessing Tiger killed her," Major Octavia is saying as she walks our way, and she hands me my side arm.

I stand there for a moment looking dumb as my gaze shifts from the weapon to the Major. When did she take my gun from me?

"We caused a brawl?" asks White.

"We didn't cause a brawl," the Major insists.

"And I didn't kill the Queen," Tiger says as she walks our way.

"Why do you still have that knife in your belly?" I ask White, because it seems to be the most important issue for the moment.

"Why didn't you kill the Queen?" the Major asks Tiger.

"Didn't need to kill her, Major," Tiger replies.

"Where is Green?" I ask, suddenly realizing she's the only absentee.

"Why do you have bruises on your face? I can see you wince every time you talk," demands the Major, a sour look on her face.

"She's got a knife in her belly," I say, pointing at white and the weapon protruding from her abdomen. I've got to avoid the Major's question somehow.

"Well if it can be safely removed, then get to it. We don't have access to surgeons here," the Major says to me, and she's both uptight and impatient. Funny, the brawling should have relieved some tension.

White and I get to work on removing the dagger from her belly. I sit her against a wall to pull the horrid thing out, and then I'm treating the remaining wound. White shows no enthusiasm or any approval for my suturing.

"It's a good thing Irwin doesn't care about my scars," she comments between passes of the needle.

"Please, it's the late twenty second century, whatever scars I leave can be glossed over later, with a laser, or however they do that now," I remind the girl. By the time I'm done closing up this belly wound White has, I have missed most all of the reporting my Lieutenant Green has given our Major.

"You killed a man, you murdered clergy, because he had a sex life?" the Major is asking her.

"I killed him because he had betrayed us, and because he had seduced uncounted adolescent girls," Lieutenant Green responds.

"Is there even an age of consent statute around here?" the Major asks, sounding exasperated, and I know she is trying to make a point about how Green has killed a man in part because his lovers were young.

"He relayed to Bellazar everything we've been doing here, Major," is Lieutenant Green's response.

The Major replies to this, yet her voice has dropped very low, and she steps closer to Green before she speaks. "That was accounted for in the plan, a lure had to be placed in the water, so to speak," Major Octavia says, and then she is turning away from Lieutenant Green. "We need to begin our exfiltration," she says to us all.

This is about the time the three Chiefs who accompanied us here approach with the message that we should get very far away from the Queen's throne, and not be seen here again for a very long time.

"We need to return to the same place as where we first arrived, just before we met with the Tsitsistas. The place is a clearing in the jungle, nearby the village of the Tsitsistas," Major Octavia tells the Chiefs, and they begin to lead us out.

Captain Malebranche looks over the recently installed *Cerberus Combat Control* system, and he still wonders if his ship will be better for it. He has no sense of his ship being better. Captain Malebranche tends to know how his ship is feeling.

"It's perfect, Mars, trust me."

Captain Malebranche looks at the sales representative from the government contractor. He looks at the man who always seems to have his slick smile ready, his clothes always perfect, and promises of grand results always flowing off his lips. "Here on the bridge of my ship I would prefer you not address me in familiar manner," Captain Malebranche replies.

"Of course, Captain, please forgive me," says the sales representative, his placating smile ever present.

"This is an untested system," says Captain Malebranche.

"Oh I assure you, Captain, the system has been subjected to the most thorough testing conceivable," says the salesman.

"You have done tests in battle?" asks the Captain.

"Well..." the salesman begins to reply.

"I am being required to deploy my vessel as soon as possible, and I am required to tolerate you installing this untested yet critical combat system without my crew being able to develop any familiarity with the mechanism, its operation or otherwise," complains Captain Malebranche, his tone low yet he sounds so very tense.

"That is the beauty of *Cerberus*, my good Captain Malebranche: you don't need any familiarity, none at all. The system is installed, it is operational. Give the command to engage your enemies, and *Cerberus* will respond. If you are attacked, then *Cerberus* will respond," the salesman explains, sounding just as if he is explaining the obvious. He has said this all before, to this very same man.

"You have installed an automated combat system on my ship without my authorization," says Captain Malebranche.

"I was authorized by your fleet procurement office to do this, and you know that's true, Captain Malebranche. You know the specifications of this system without my needing offer explanation. I understand your feathers being ruffled. This is a grand ship. The *Infernal Storm* is one of the most prestigious battleships in all the Bellazar fleet, and your job is to take care of her. Your duty is to oversee her actions in battle with deadly efficiency, and your ultimate mandate is victory at all costs. Do not fear, Captain Malebranche, *Cerberus* is victory," the salesman declares.

"This *thing* employs men as living processors. You call it *Cerberus* because three human minds are slaved to the system, their bodies installed as if hardware," Captain Malebranche says, waving a hand toward *Cerberus*.

"Such a consideration isn't really pertinent, not to one such as you, Captain Malebranche. That is to say, you really don't care about these three men, do you?" replies the salesman.

"I don't know these three men you have made a part of your machine, yet now they are a part of my ship, and that must concern me. I don't know their names, so how can I enter them in the ship's log as new crewmen? They wear helmets that serve as contact points for data entry and transfer. How can I know them as men if I can't look them in the eye?" asks Captain Malebranche.

"They are not men, my Captain. They are wetware processors. They are equipment, not crewmen. They are objects of function, not people serving the mission. These three *were* men, now they are units, *component units* of the *Cerberus Combat System*," the salesman explains, waving his arms with flourish.

"It would have helped if you had put shirts on them: Shirts and pants, because it would be easier to look at these three men as only objects if we couldn't see their chest hair, their naked legs, or their nipples. Also, in spite of the fact I can't look them in the eye for the headgear, the rest of their faces are obviously twisted masks of pain. What am I to make of that?" asks Captain Malebranche.

"Captain, make victory for Bellazar; make many great victories," says the salesman, now obviously losing his patience with Captain Malebranche. Yet he still wears the smile of a salesman.

Captain Malebranche wants to respond. He's still looking at the freakish monstrosity that has been installed at the center of his ship's command deck, and at the three men ensconced within the *Cerberus*, their bodies apparently twisted with pain, and their faces warped in agony. The words of rebuff Captain Malebranche wishes to deliver to the detestable salesman have reached the tip of his tongue when klaxons sound and sailors everywhere spring into action.

Infernal Storm is in the last stages of preparing to get underway, action orders of high eminence having been delivered that very morning. Crewmen await orders to retract all gangway positions, and to cast off all mooring points. A general announcement is then heard by all:

"This is the officer of the deck, ship's plan of the day calls for Infernal Storm to be under way within the hour, and all visitors must be off the ship within five minutes!"

"That's my cue, Captain Malebranche. I will see you at the parade held in your honor when you return," the salesman says, and then he is quick stepping from the command deck, and headed off the ship.

Captain Mars Malebranche turns away from his new combat system and looks out at his busy bridge crew. He knows battle is probably where they are being sent, and the Captain already knows whatever they might find, he is to take control where it is they go.

All of a sudden the Major has us running: the four Soldier Girls, and the three chiefs who have volunteered as our guides. Well, the Chiefs don't have to run because we can probably find our way back to the extraction zone without their help. We are heading for that very spot, going as the crow flies. Yet two of these chiefs have proposed marriage to us, have they not? These men must show themselves manly and worthy to be husbands. So we run, and the Chiefs run with us. I think the Major had us running mostly so she could see what these

Chiefs were made of, if they would stick it out. Otherwise it is just mission imperative that prompts this intensive exercise, and I don't want to think that could be the cause of it.

I know we are soon to leave this planet, and never would I or any of the rest of us have actually entertained a marriage proposal from a single man of this world. Yeah, they are all sweetness and light when the courtship begins, yet God only knows what dreary desperation is destined once they have you in their hut wearing their band of matrimony.

No, for us the real question is what is to come? What happens next? After we make the trek back to our landing site what are we going to do? Naturally the *Dowager's Daughter* is coming for us, yet just how is unknown. The Major knows, and I think it must be sure that Captain Malloy already knows how our extraction is to be achieved, yet I and the other soldier girls? We lowly grunts, we are to know nothing, we are told nothing, not until it is required, a timely necessity.

We ultimately find our way to the clearing, and once there Major Octavia opens her own drop pod and draws out a hand portable radio with a rather impressive aerial. We watch her use the unit.

"Ground one to orbit," Major Octavia calls.

"Orbit, go Ground one," a voice responds and I know I am hearing Captain Malloy.

"Orbit, we are looking for extraction, please advise?" Major Octavia calls back.

"Zone is hot, Ground one. Fire fills the sky as devils dance," Captain Malloy transmits.

"*Fire fills the sky as devils dance*? None of that is our established code," says the Major, as she gives the radio an odd look. Then she keys the radio to transmit: "Orbit, Ground one seeks extract, please advise?"

"Eggs before they hatch, Ground one, going to market before the gate is open," Captain Malloy radios back.

Major Octavia puts away the radio and when she looks at us her face is stern like Medusa. No one cracks wise. No one says a word. When she gives us directions we follow, and when she speaks we listen, hard. "Right team, time for final briefing, or as close to it as we can come. Hostiles are confirmed in the area, and we have to move beyond them to reach our destination. Bellazar has moved a considerable asset into the area because they know about us, and because Bellazar won't give up influence on this area without losing a considerable asset. Everyone is going back into their drop pods, and sealing them tight. We are going out the same way we came in."

This is when one of the chiefs suddenly looking very sad asks Major Octavia a question: "Does this mean our wedding is off?"

Chapter Eight

When he read the orders that had just come in Colonel Brackenbok nearly fell out of his chair. Colonel Brackenbok nearly fell off his own feet when he stood and first attempted to walk as his eyes would stray to the orders he now carried in hand. Colonel Brackenbok, as he stood with the new orders in hand before the Commodore, he stumbled over his own words once, then twice, and with a last gasp of desperation, the Colonel handed the printed orders over to his Commodore.

Taking the orders, the Commodore reads. Having read, she looks to her first officer, not the Colonel, her chief of staff, and most able assistant, not the Colonel. Speaking to this man, the Commodore says: "You know our course and heading, Colonel," and then she hands the orders back to Colonel Brackenbok. The good Colonel is about to call out the new course and heading to the helmsman when the Commodore interrupts him. "I need a direct line of secure communication with the battle cruiser *Juno*," Commodore Pretorian calls out.

The radiomen on the command deck scramble to comply with the orders of their Commodore.

Within moments a radioman is calling out: "Commodore, Battlecruiser *Juno* is on the line, and awaiting your word."

Commodore Pretorian picks up a headset, and adjusting the boom microphone, she begins to speak: "*Juno*, this is *Hera*. I have new orders, and I now require you to deploy both your squadrons of torpedo bombers. The heavy bombers are to be armed, category five heaviest munitions, and the bombers are to take up station to ride an extended warp field. When we bring the bombers with us through the warp field they must be prepared to engage hostiles the moment we exit warp transition." She can tell that no one on the other end of the line is happy to hear these orders. There are several moments of silence until a reply is heard.

"Encrypt and transmit a conformation code," the *Juno* responds.

Commodore Pretorian is forced to take a moment to pause, and then she is tapping console keys, entering her conformation code.

"Transmit co-sign," the Juno transmits.

Commodore Pretorian complies with this instruction, and then she further complies with the requirement to transmit a check-sum. Once all authorizations are in place the *Juno* begins to launch her Torpedo Bombers, and those ships begin the work of taking up station keeping positions close under the belly of the *Hera*. Commodore Pretorian looks to her first officer, and says: "Begin the process of coalescing the warp field."

****

I don't really understand the method of extraction we are using until I put some facts together. We are working to rig the drop pods with harness and cables that connect to a rig that is fixed with auto-inflate balloons. One by one I assist the Major as she places the Soldier Girls into their individual drop pods, and then Major Octavia rigorously checks and double checks the seals and locks. She makes me watch her at every step of the way, and confirm what she does. The moment seems dry, procedural, yet this is the true evidence of how much she cares about us, because I know where this is all going. If the pods are not sealed proper, then we inside are going to be dead. I'm the last one to enter pod with the Major's assistance, and just before she closes me in the last thing she bothers to say is: "No matter what happens you must reach *Janus*. Think of nothing else from here on, only *Janus*, you and Green must reach *Janus*. The technicians will do the rest." Then she's closed me in. No time to beg or demand explanation. Just the command to *reach Janus*, and that's it. The pod interior feels cramped, overly enclosed, and yet I am sharing space only with my little scout carbine. Tiger is taller than I, and she shares her pod with her sniper rifle. The thing is taller than Tiger herself, and had to be broken down into three pieces to be placed into the pod. I insert an audio bud into my ear, yet there is nothing on our unit radio to listen to until the Major has herself sealed into her own pod, with the help of the local chiefs, and God help us if they botched it. The Major is more vulnerable to the hazards of the void than are her indomitable Soldier Girls.

Once the Major is inside her pod she begins an effort to make contact with *Dowager's Daughter* and Captain Malloy. From what I hear it can be discerned the ship is coming in hot, actually *on fire*. The atmospheric angle of descent was wrong, the heat build-up too much, and Captain Malloy is doing harm to his ship in his effort to recover us Soldier Girls. What's the hurry? The fact that he is in contact signals the Major to remotely activate the balloons, and they carry far into the sky that tremendously rugged ring and cable rig that's attached to every harness on each pod. Captain Malloy drops through the sky flying as fast as he can, and still be able to maneuver through the atmosphere. The deck apes drop a tail hook, and even though this should be impossible without hours of practice, they catch us, and then we are flying. The tail hook yanks us off the ground with brutal force. The sensation of sudden upward lift is jarring. There is no telling how much additional gravitational force we are subjected to, and I want to believe we didn't exceed supersonic velocity until after Captain Malloy was flying outside atmosphere again, except the easiest way to escape gravity is to fly as fast as you can. Obviously the *Dowager's Daughter* is capable of super-sonic flight. I suppose at some point my senses simply could no longer register the weight of what we were being subjected to, and I was, for want of a better word, numb. I still heard Captain Malloy over the radio. I heard him order his crew to abandon ship while we were still in the atmosphere. I heard him talk about 'running the blockade' and hoping the ship he called *Infernal Storm* would ignore our one small cargo carrier. We moved beyond the atmosphere of *Aborto Espontáneo Blanco* and Captain Malloy commented how the fires were mostly out and the deck apes were all gone. While we were now out of a gravity field, Captain Malloy was at full thrust, he has the ship throttle all the way open, so to speak. We were streaking across the starry sky with Captain Malloy asking *where is it*, and *where will it appear*. Only the *"it"* he expected wasn't the 'it' that came into being.

There was some kind of battleship in the area when Captain Malloy picked us up, and this ship had deployed interceptors and corvettes in patrols to respond to anything like us. Just as the hostiles in the area began to take notice of our presence something that seems far more important appears as a warp field opens to admit something more fearsome than any idol curiosity. The opening warp field allowed for another ship to appear and from what I hear Captain Malloy say the second ship was no match in sheer bulk for the first, yet this second ship seemed to have whole wings of fighters deployed from the moment it appeared. I hear Captain Malloy comment on the stark visual difference in the two ships. The one was "red, and seems to slough off red" as if shedding skin or possibly it's bleeding. The second is blue and white, sleek with cleanest lines. The second ship was immaculate, and was absolutely the image of a raptor given mechanical form, and still majestically beautiful.

The *Infernal Storm* had appeared from a sudden red crack in the sky, and from that red fissure the *Infernal Storm* was a pale red dreadnought moving at stately pace that at no moment betrayed her deadly prowess. When Captain Malebranche had arrived in system, and then taken up orbit around *Aborto Espontáneo Blanco* he'd sensed nothing troubling, at least not for a while. Then he felt his ship telling him the enemy was near. *Infernal Storm* had intuition all her own, and her fury always followed her notions of where the battle was to be found. There was an independently chartered cargo carrier climbing up from the planet surface, and usually that meant nothing. Except this planet has no space port because Bellazar had yet to send engineers and the construction crews to build the port. It was still in the planning stages and had to be cleared in negotiations with Queen Semiramis, the only recognized planetary ruler. The word was the political leaders and the diplomatic corps were both enamored of the alien leader known as Queen Semiramis. They found something in her personal qualities quite endearing, and they were willing to indulge her whims. The identification of the independent cargo carrier was suspect. An independent carrier all the way out here in a system ostensibly claimed by Bellazar, what was it doing? These were trivial considerations when one recognized the velocity, trajectory, and reckless flying on display. Also the cargo carrier seemed to be towing something, objects, relatively tinny objects, and it all failed to add up. It didn't make sense unless you considered the possibility that something underhanded was in progress. So Captain Malebranche ordered interceptors and gunships to investigate, just a few will be diverted for now.

This was the moment the battle cruiser *Hera* appeared and with her the two wings of borrowed Torpedo Bombers. The *Hera* transitions near the planetary nadi; that is close proximity to *the North Pole*. Commodore Pretorian ordered her ship to action stations, and she demanded her vessel be at battle conditions within just moments. On that same instant Commodore Pretorian ordered the bombers to attack the *Infernal Storm*. Then she ordered the launch of every interceptor and attack ship under her command. Everyone onboard the *Hera* responded as ordered, all save one.

The executive officer, Colonel Brackenbok, he was being inundated on his personal, and confidential feed, with red flags, security warnings and other flash message traffic requiring his examination. Colonel Brackenbok was at his action station, a console dedicated for his personal use, and he was going through a series of confirmations and examinations of transactions that security protocols required he clear before he could do anything else. Literally there was such a backlog of security violations, transgressions, and suspect actions to suddenly appear that the executive officer's workstation was being rendered useless until he looked over everything, battle or no, combat or not.

When *Infernal Storm* registered the Arcadian Command Carrier newly arrived in the area, Captain Malebranche ordered his ship to full defensive posture. He ordered the launch of every fighter craft his ship had to offer. He ordered every weapon manned, primed and ready. It eased Captain Malebranche when he saw the *Cerberus* Combat Control System operating not just well; it actually seemed to be functioning flawlessly. Now nothing was being done about the independent cargo carrier, yet what needed to be done about one possible smuggler when three waves of torpedo bombers were on their attack run, deployed from a warship of nearly equal size and tonnage? The *Cerberus* was supervising the defensive weaponry of the *Infernal Storm*, and many of those torpedo bombers suffered crippling blows. A number of the bombers were destroyed outright, and yet some got through, if only to deliver their payload of munitions, and then be destroyed. As torpedoes were reported detonating upon the ship, Captain Malebranche stood silent, stern, and only issuing commands when necessary. The ship's armor absorbed most of the torpedo damage. There were moments when a torpedo struck a lucky spot, and penetrated the ship, destroying something of importance. Yet *Infernal*

Storm is a true behemoth, and capable to absorb copious amounts of damage.

Captain Malebranche was being patient. He knew it would take time to maneuver his ship to a range and position where he could directly engage the enemy vessel from Arcadia. Also, Captain Malebranche knew at any moment one of his own fighters would probably report a crippling strike against the Arcadian. Captain Malebranche had deployed only two types of craft: stealth interceptors, and heavy gunships. That's all he had access to, because that is Bellazar strategic doctrine, either you are sneaking up on your enemy so as to allow you to strike a death blow, or you attack openly with a frontal assault of such strength you will strike only a death blow. Captain Malebranche had launched his *Silentio Nox* fighters with their state of the art stealth fields, and his *Mors Lotus* gunships, with firepower possibly equal to some corvettes and other escorts. The fighters helped in part to protect *Infernal Storm* from the torpedo bombers while the gunships advanced toward the enemy cruiser.

Did the *Hera* perceive her danger?

Once the *Hera* is fully engaged she begins to take a serious beating. *Hera* was getting hit hard by the corvettes from the *Infernal Storm*, and people on board the Arcadia battle cruiser wonder just how big a fight they have blustered into? *Hera* shakes and shudders with impacts as invisible interceptors strafe the hull, seeking out vulnerable points. Crewmembers stumble, and many are thrown from their feet when a corvette manages to hit home with their mass driver weapon. This is literally the hammering of giant spikes into the *Hera*, delivering simple yet effective kinetic energy as a weapon. The impacts cause Colonel Brackenbok to struggle as he sits his action station, examining security flash messages that have commandeered his attention. Everything he is being shown at the moment is a series of indicators telling him with overwhelming confidence that someone onboard *Hera*, someone with key command authority is a mole.

A *mole*: a kind of spy that infiltrates an organization working to subvert and undermine that entity from within. High Command has only just now determined that an enemy agent has been inserted into the *Hera* chain of command, and that agent has for a long time now been manipulating the ship to the place, and position it is presently in. Colonel Brackenbok is on the verge of an anxiety attack as he is being forced to track down anomalies in message authorization codes and erroneous identifiers while his ship is being battered by outside enemies.

"Do not stop fighting! We will stand or fall here and now!" shouts out Commodore Pretorian from nearby where the Colonel sits examining the trail that will lead him to the officer that has subverted his ship's true mission. Then it all comes clear. The algorithm tracking the errant identifiers that allowed a spy to infiltrate the command structure of the *Hera* produces a name, the name of the officer who has been exclusively employing those identifiers. Only a few moments later Colonel Brackenbok is able to concur with the computer generated indictment, and he prepares himself to present formal impeachment. Anxious, yet stern and steady, Colonel Brackenbok stands. He walks to within ten paces of the suspect officer, and Colonel Brackenbok declares: "Commodore Pretorian! I relieve you of command under charges of high treason, and being an agent of the enemy!"

This moment was accompanied by a *Mors Lotus* corvette discharging its mass driver weapon with perfect aim. The projectile flies through space losing none of its velocity for having traveled through void and vacuum. The projectile strikes the command bridge of the *Hera* battle cruiser and destroys a great many objects. Yet only one death will be confirmed from this weapons impact. The mass driver strike utterly destroys the body and thus takes the life of Colonel Brackenbok.

The woman known as Commodore Pretorian looks around. No one had really heard the accusation or charges leveled against her. Yet it doesn't matter. They saw their Executive Officer annihilated, and now *Hera* is in a fight she can't win. Despite her words, Commodore Pretorian was never here to see this fight through to the end, only to bring this considerable asset to the field of contention. Now the role of *Commodore Pretorian* is done, and the woman must make her exit.

For Patrice her time as *Commodore Pretorian* is over, and her mission priority is her own personal survival. Several crewmembers of the *Hera* are left dumbfounded when they see their Commodore flee the bridge without giving any further orders. Several moments pass and then someone responding to indicator lights at their action station asks: "Why is Commodore Pretorian leaving the ship on her personal skiff?"

Captain Malloy begins to slow his ship to take up station keeping at just the position pre-appointed. The precious drop pods he tows will be jostled a bit, yet if the plan works out, it will only be for a few moments. Then it is as if the sky explodes before Jack Malloy, a detonation of purple, as if a storm of static and lightning is generated spontaneously. The field of purple lightning grows, and Captain Malloy is forced to worry that he is too close. Then from the purple lightning field begins to emerge an enormous mass of chaos. Like a sea urchin ten thousand meters in circumference and displacing ten thousand tons the *Void Helkein* emerges from the purple lightning field, transitioning from warp space into real space. In that one instant nearly everything happening around the planet *Aborto Espontáneo Blanco* is brought to a pause.

On board the *Hera*, where the crew has lost their two senior officers within moments, people are absolutely stunned. They don't know how to react at all to this newcomer. Those who are manning defensive weapons continue to do so, unaware of the destroyed command structure. Those fighting fires or sealing ruptures in the hull continue as they have been, not knowing that quite possibly an irresistible monster has entered the fray.

The *Infernal Storm* has been enduring, and returning battle damage with stoic, even grim determination. Captain Malebranche has found this battle odd from the onset. A ship like the *Hera* should never have engaged his *Infernal Storm*. Not on her own, not without support. Even with the two additional wings of attack craft the *Hera* should not have come to this fight alone. It is as if the Arcadians have sacrificed the vessel, and Captain Malebranche knows the Arcadians are too smart for that, they would never be so insipid as to throw away in desperation so valuable an asset as the capitol ship

Hera. Although *Infernal Storm* will leave this engagement with many deep scars, the Bellazar capitol ship, perhaps the most fearsome super dreadnought in the Bellazar fleet, it will surely end this day victorious. Indeed, *Infernal Storm* will likely end the day with a kill of the *Hera*. Then the inexplicable happens. Captain Malebranche sees the explosion of warp lightning. He sees the field of static take form, massive, impossibly immense, and from out of that warp field Mars Malebranche sees impossibility. Captain Malebranche identifies what he sees as a Void Helkein, and yet he can't believe what he sees of it: the anomaly exiting the warp of interstellar transition, and moving as if being consciously maneuvered. A Void Helkein does not maneuver, it drifts mindless, a hazard to all that may encounter it. Whatever is going on, whatever may have brought the Void Helkein here, Captain Malebranche makes the decision to ignore the anomaly for the time being and concentrate on destroying his original target: the *Hera*. If not already in her death throws, the *Hera* is soon to be a dead hulk.

What has nobody noticed? What is that upon the sea urchin that is called the *Void Helkein*? Sea urchins do not have mites; they do not suffer such parasites do they? Yet from the spines of Void Helkein, spines that are actually up until recently long abandoned space faring vessels, many of them warships, and other armed vessels, now from these *warship spines* emerge things so tinny they might as well be the smallest of mites. Yet these are not insect parasites, these are the *Lupus Miles*. They are soldiers and they are wolves. They are robotic attack automatons long discarded, rediscovered and reinvigorated with a new and crucial duty. Originally created for ship-to-ship assaults, the Lupus Miles have mostly languished where they were discarded. Now they have been given purpose again, a stern mistress has returned the *Lupus Miles* to their original and true calling. Well, they aren't attacking another ship. The Wolf-Soldiers are actually recovering the objects in tow from one ship, and returning those objects to the soldier's point of origin: the Void Helkein. Uncoupling the central ring from the tail hook of the *Dowager's Daughter*, the Lupus Miles push off from the skin of one ship, returning to the Void Helkein. Indeed, the Lupus Miles accomplish their mission without anyone noticing, no one except those who have been awaiting their return.

The most horrible sight greets my eyes when the drop pod is finally reopened, and it takes all the discipline I have to not react with open revulsion, or outright violence. Indeed, that most horrible of sights? An overly bossy gang of technicians billowing for Green and me to exit our drop pods and follow these repellent men to the thing they call *Janus*. Also there is at least a half dozen wolf headed robots standing about looking like blood thirsty muscle men. One of them all black in color is constantly muttering *'I am Kveldulf'* and *'I am the night'* like some daft nutter. No time to gawk, the technicians won't have it, so Green and I are up, on our feet and being ushered at the quick step to a compartment I manage to recognize.

This is the expansive chamber with what I took to be luxuriant command couches. As we enter I notice the form of a woman almost entirely concealed in the shadows far off from where everyone else is at work. Whoever that gal is, she so reminds me of the Widow. I mean the way she stands, watching what happens; it reminds me of just the body language I have seen in Morganti. This time I also notice the couches have gaps where the back of your neck would lie as you recline. "Why do they still face away from one another?" I ask as I am hustled to one couch and Green to the other.

"That's how it works, that's how it has always worked," a technician says, yet he seems distracted. It's the Chief Technician I think, the one who was bragging up this thing last we were here. The Major chased us out once she heard that boy talk to us about what this thing really may be. I should have known then it would be important in the future. Whatever the Major keeps secret, whatever knowledge she guards against us gaining, it must always be a part of an unfolding plan that she fears someone might betray.

"Topical anesthetic?" I hear one technician call out.

"No time!" shouts the Chief Technician.

"This will hurt, but I'm sure your type deals with it fine," says the Technician at my side.

"Your type? You cheeky sod!" I shout in his face, then he and another are taking hold of my arms, and just as I think to resist the Major is here, shouting directions.

"Let them do as they must, our mission depends on it!" the Major calls out as she enters this chamber. Her tone is commanding, and yet I can also hear how she is pleading with us, Green and me. Then I see a technician with a scalpel.

"What's that?" I demand.

"We have to establish the full range of connections," another technician says.

"Just turn off your pain receptors!" the Chief Technician shouts out as he works at the central console while Green and I are about to be butchered.

"I can talk them through the process! It isn't something they have been briefed on before!" White is shouting as she follows the Major into the room.

"We don't have time! No pain killer, nothing! Cut them! Cut them now and complete the input and connection process!" shouts that awful Chief Technician. I know who I'm going to be having an in depth private chat with once this is all over.

With men holding our arms and legs, other men begin to cut at us. Two cuts at each side of our brow, and two cuts on either side of the back of our neck. Now I have blood running down the sides of my face, and down my back. This makes for such a nice accent to this deeply personal violation. It seems there are contact points at these locations, just under the skin, and they insert plugs with some haste. Was this some aspect of my construct I'd long forgotten for lack of employment? As soon as we are all hooked up we go limp. Parts of us simply cease to function, even if temporarily. I do not see with my eyes, now I see with the vast sensor arrays available to the *Void Helkein*. I barely sense it as our bodies are laid down upon the comfy couches, and something strange happens to our thoughts.

"We are the command module," I or we think. It's funny how I can *feel* Green as if she is just beside me.

"We are the command nodes," she or I think.

"We command the Void Helkein."

"We are divided, and we are one."

"They are in sync! Their psyche is now a duel union!" the Chief Technician shouts with too much glee.

"You have to direct the Void Helkein to attack the *Infernal Storm*, or we are all going to die!" someone tells us, I have no idea who.

"Is it working?" I hear someone ask, and I start to believe Morganti may be here.

"We must have target solutions."

"I will target my missiles."

"I will launch my torpedoes."

Then I sense a vast number of highly complicated equations running through my head, math I didn't know I was capable of, and yet *I or we* are doing all of the calculations. Actually I sense we are targeting both of the major warships in the area, and yet the munitions directed at the further ship, the smaller ship, are less for damage, and more for countermeasures. We have identified the further ship as Arcadian, and we seem to know we don't want to do that one any more harm than necessary. We clearly and mercilessly aim for the nearer ship, the one we mark *Infernal Storm*, a capitol ship of the Bellazar Navy. So while flares and chaff bombs fly at the ship labeled *Hera*, fully armed ordinance screams its way toward *Infernal Storm*.

Captain Malebranche reads the change in the battle situation. The monstrous newcomer is no ally, their attack conclusive evidence of their nature. Add to that the *Hera* having become listless, nearly dead in space, and Captain Malebranche makes a quick decision.

"Ahead one third, Helm, revise course forty-five degrees to starboard. Weapons, adjust your target!"

Captain Malebranche was determined to fight as long as he can, and yet his ship has been battered, bruised, and even wounded by the *Hera*. Can the *Infernal Storm* be expected to face this second, new and fresh enemy? If not for the damage his vessel has already suffered, if not for the anomalies of this battle, it would be of little concern, not a question at all. Why did the Arcadians even choose to come here and fight, and why have they fought so poorly? Why has only one vessel escaped from the *Hera*, and thrusting straight toward the newcomer? Actually the thing doesn't fly straight, it flies like a maniac, and if it weren't so small and seeming insignificant Captain Malebranche would order it shot out of the sky. Then there is the matter of the rogue cargo carrier. Captain Malebranche has ordered it destroyed, and with easy justification: the cargo carrier is on the attack. It's actually heavily armed, fast, and far more maneuverable than originally anticipated. Why the thing is attacking real warships is unknown, and will never be answered because Captain Malebranche has ordered the rogue cargo ship annihilated.

The *Hera* is managing to limp away from the scene. Critically damaged, and with many key crewmen killed or missing, one man from among the officers takes charge and gives the orders that have the only hope of saving the ship. What fighters can be recovered, have been. Now *Hera* turns, and begins to move away from *Infernal Storm* and the *Void Helkein* as fast as she can. With a command intended to shunt power to the most vital systems, the Executive Officer's work station loses all power without the benefit of proper shutdown. This means the mass of evidence showing that Commodore Pretorian was actually a spy who brought *Hera* to this battle under false pretenses is probably lost, or at least corrupted forever. Really, there was an actual *preponderance*. There is no regard for any of that now. The *Hera* must survive, that is the imperative of any engagement: bring the ship home.

Captain Malloy has his concussion cannons set to continuous fire. He has his helm set so that his ship flies inerrant, straight toward the *Infernal Storm*. This is when Captain Malloy really begins to scramble. The ship is burnt, broken, and it is amazing that any portions of the combat or propulsion systems still work. So Jack is rushing to get into his environmental suit with the helmet. Then, climbing into the escape boat, Jack seals the portal, and jettisons himself into space. From a distance he watches the ship that was his home for years, the vessel of his rehabilitation, destroyed.

Captain Malebranche is a merciless warrior. In the moment he realizes there is a threat, he reacts, and that reaction is always lethal. When the rogue cargo ship is detected flying straight at the *Infernal Storm*, Captain Malebranche orders it destroyed without hesitation. This is both wise and unfortunate as the firepower necessary to destroy the new target is sufficient to allow a good portion of the missile and torpedo attack from the old target to get through: the *Void Helkein* is going to cripple the *Infernal Storm*. The *Dowager's Daughter* even in her youth never could have survived any portion of the fury *Infernal Storm* now concentrates on her. The cargo ship, reconfigured for so many secret missions so many times, now old, broken, and burnt beyond repair, shows just how hard it is to destroy something made well, yet ultimately the *Dowager's Daughter* is shattered.

Nearly a half dozen missiles or torpedoes managed to pass the defensive screen meant to protect *Infernal Storm*. The impact of these weapons has caused scattered, large fires on at least three decks. The fires are growing, and become nearly out of control. Captain Malebranche is no longer on the offensive. Having destroyed one target, the enemy managed to pass through a dagger and stab him in the belly. That is the effect: it's just as if Mars himself has been wounded. Captain Malebranche has turned his ship from an attack posture on a closing vector with his target, to a defensive posture retreating from the enemy. The Void Helkein is larger than first estimated, and able to bring to bear far more fire power than originally anticipated. With his ship burning, with hull breaches wreathed by flames, Captain Malebranche orders the *Infernal Storm* to withdraw.

"We have not destroyed the target," we call out from the *Janus*.

"We must pursue," we continue.

"Those are not your orders," someone says to us, and we have to think for a moment. Is the Major making address to us? "Take up a defensive position in orbit of Aborto Espontáneo Blanco," the Major commands. Yes, this is the Major, we are sure of that now.

"We will orbit the planet," we decide, and somehow our minds begin the work of maneuvering the vast, nearly unimaginable bulk of the *Void Helkein* toward the planet.

"Prepare to hardwire and lock them down as the permanent central operating system for the Void Helkein," the Chief Technician orders.

Part Three
The Unforeseen Extension

Chapter Nine

Instantly I'm searching, trying to find some way to *see* what is happening. I can't open my eyes, or perhaps my eyes have been shut down as part of the integration with the *Janus* control system. I can't move my body: again it is as if parts of me have been taken offline to attend the greater tasks. While I am distracted with just how much I am not capable of, Green has found a closed circuit camera that looks right at the room, the very spot where we lie helpless before this squadron of technicians that seem to see us as pieces of equipment for their experiments. White stands near the Major. The Chief Technician is still at his central console examining the readings, and insisting his orders be followed. Tiger has shown up. When did Tiger show up? The woman in the shadows is still in the shadows, and when the Major looks her way, there is a nod of the head. As if following some explicit command the Major draws my side arm... wait, when did she take my gun? This is the second time, yeah? The Major has my gun, and she aims it at the Chief Technician.

The man is determined and unflappable. He tries to bark his orders at his crew of techs, and they might have listened. Then the Major has shot him in the back, or rather, she shoots him right in the tail bone. He falls, and lies still. Not dead, just crippled. The Major looks at White and all the Technicians, and says: "Get my officers out of that rig and onto their feet," and then looking at White, the Major says: "Sew them good, minimize the scars."

Contact points are disconnected. We go from fully plugged in, literally an absolute immersive control of the massive construct called the *Void Helkein*, and then we are falling into darkness. Later, I don't know how long, I wake to the odd sensation that someone is fondling me. When I'm able to open my own eyes I see White looking terribly worried as she examines my wounds. Then she notices I'm awake.

"Look, there is a problem: the technician who cut you was the sloppier of the two, and he wasn't using a true surgical scalpel. I'm sorry, so sorry, but you are going to have scars, two small scars running along both sides of your head and the back of your neck. They will resemble the scars exhibited by members of a fencing or duelist club. I know that's little consolation, yet there is only so much I can do. When we have time later I will personally take you to the plastic surgeon," the girl is explaining with sad, concerned eyes and an emphatic tone of voice.

I look at Green, and she looks back at me. If there were not stitches in her fair flesh then I would have no way of knowing she'd been injured.

"I was just lucky to get the better cutter," she says to me.

"No, I'm glad you did. I couldn't bear the thought of your visage marred in any way," I tell her, and then I worry what I said came out wrong. Really, I am just so tired. It's been a long day. Green gives me that subtle yet perfect smile of hers and I stop with my apprehensions.

The *Void Helkein* was moved into the best stable orbit of the planet *Aborto Espontáneo Blanco* that can be achieved, and apparently Green and I did that while plugged into the bizarre *Janus* contraption. Most of the technicians are looking at Green and me with admiration. I don't know why, yet later I will learn it's because of how we were able to use the *Janus* system so well. At later time one of them will say: *'the two of you operated Janus at least two geometric steps beyond our expectations.'* Well, we did manage to beat a Bellazar super dreadnought.

Things liven up when Captain Malloy appears, and... then it gets shocking. We see the Major run to him, *she actually runs to the man, and throws her arms around him.* Even from a distance we hear her call his name.

"Jack, I was so worried," she tells him, and I have never heard so much emotion in her voice. Not like this, not that I can recall.

Another woman enters the room behind Captain Malloy, and as she walks past the couple in their embrace, she is heard to say: "I knew that would make you happy." It seems mysterious to me that the woman seems to be dressed in a kind of naval uniform, as if a flag officer.

The Major instantly breaks her contact with the Captain, and she is glaring a wicked glare at this woman. "Patrice!" the Major says, pretty much spitting the name out as if to say the name leaves her mouth full of bitter taste.

Everyone watches Patrice cross the floor heading toward the woman in the shadows. This is when the woman in the shadows steps forward to show herself for the first time. Stepping forward, she is revealed to be just who I suspected, and I'm sure you guessed: Morganti Giovani Bastille, the Widow of the Market Town.

"Is my transportation ready?" Patrice asks.

"You just commandeered an Admiral's gig. Do you really want to change horse midstream?" Morganti asks, a sly smile creeping its way onto her face.

"I don't want to be caught flying around in stolen property. You tend to prefer I keep the lowest of profile," Patrice responds, she presents her own smile, and then she goes on: "Besides, my brief was that I'm to take a fresh transport from here when the mission is complete."

Morganti raises a hand, snapping a finger, and an underling manifests to guide Patrice to her requested fresh transport. Goodness, look at that man, all dressed in silky white cream pajamas two sizes too big for him, and he is a real skinny boy. The Major never stops staring hate at Patrice, and none of us, not a one has ever figured out what is behind it. Seriously, the Major is wearing her dark glasses, just like she *always* is, and still you can see the enmity boiling up from within her. I'm not going to ask, are you?

Then Morganti points a finger at us, Green and me, and speaking to White, she give a command: "Those two are on orders to pound the sandman for the next twelve hours. In about twenty four hours I will sit with all of you, and as a group we will debrief."

So that young girl we call White, in her role as medical officer, she puts us to bed, and does so with sedatives she distributes. The pills keep Green and me asleep for the next twelve hours. We wake, we stretch, and we eat. Also we dress. I don't want you to think we went naked to an important meeting with the boss of our boss. Funny thing, when I reach for my gun belt I find my weapon there, in holster, and looking as if the gun has been cleaned and oiled just within the hour. I suppose that is the Major's way of saying *'sorry for borrowing your stuff without permission'* or some such. I supposed I'll never find out why she felt it necessary to borrow my sidearm, in particular *my* sidearm.

We sit for our group debrief. It's one of the biggest meetings I've ever been a part of, unless you consider that time I was on trial. Don't ask now, it's another story for another time. Didn't I tell that one already? If not yet, do not fret, Old Mother Black will someday tell the tale. As I was saying we sit for our big meeting with our boss, our ultimate boss: Morganti Giovani Bastille, the Widow of the Market Town. She sits across from *everyone*, and though she is one of the smallest women I've ever encountered she's always had the kind of presence that makes you feel tinny. The chamber within the *Void Helkein* where we have this meeting is well furnished, and it seems all the stuff must have been brought onboard just for the purpose of this meeting. The chairs all appear to be made of real wood, and have plush cushions of green velvet on the seats, arms and backrest. It seems as if the Widow is in a larger, taller chair than the rest of us. Her chair can't be too much bigger or else the small woman's feet just wouldn't reach the floor. Maybe she's had her people give all the rest of us undersize furniture? The table before us, this table that sits lengthwise between us and the Widow it seems tall for a table of its type or at least it does once we sit in the chairs. I actually don't know how this sort of thing is supposed to work, never having done it much, yet I find the seating arrangement odd, and I have to wonder who set the chairs out in the way we find them. The Major and the Captain sit together, side by side, and directly opposite the Widow. I sit beside White, a few steps behind the Major, while Green and Tiger sit a few steps behind Captain Malloy. Once we are all seated Morganti convenes the debrief meeting.

"Well, for the present it seems we are successful," she begins. A moment is allowed to pass before she goes on. "By success I mean that I and my corporate allies now enjoy exclusive access to all the mineral resources of *Aborto Espontáneo Blanco*. Indeed, the planet has no apparent external trading partners. While you know that I have worked to overturn monopolies, we are at this time a *de facto* monopoly here in the area of Aborto Espontáneo Blanco. Of course this is happening with an entity that thinks of themselves as having little to no need of external trading partners, Queen Semiramis in particular having adopted isolationist attitude. That's not a worry: we always plan to go around the local authorities when they chose to pose as an impediment to our efforts concerning the capture of market share."

I'm thinking there is so much wrong with what she just said, even though most of it is correct. What do I know? I'm just boots on the ground, or a machine plugged into another machine, depending on our mission requirements. We have to wait and hear what the Widow has to say about when the big boys come back: Bellazar and Arcadia. Those are the interstellar nation-states we have probably enraged to the edge of all reason, right? My private thoughts are suspended when Morganti continues.

"Major, the alliances you made while on the planet surface will go a long way to help us. Although we will have to speak another time about the way you heedlessly spurn marriage proposals made in the best of good faith," Morganti says, and after uttering that last bit she lets us see her smile. For a moment there I see a little girl on the edge of a giggle fit. She so wants to laugh at her own joke. We smile in return, and laugh because we certainly have been given permission. Then Morganti goes on: "It is true we surely have taken actions that probably offend the two empires. Arcadia has nearly lost one of their proudest capitol ships and Bellazar has suffered the crippling of what we hear is their most imposing super dreadnought. Indeed, a ship like *Infernal Storm* could serve as a system wide monitor by itself if need be, while *Hera* is traditionally the lead ship in a battle group that usually is considered beyond challenge. That's why we have developed this asset: the *Void Helkein*. Let them return, and they will feel the wrath of this fully functional battle station. I do not expect the Arcadians to return soon in any effort to avenge their loss. They suffered principally at the hands of Bellazar, their old enemy. The Arcadian struggle of the moment is to get back home in one piece. I can't even say for certain if they will be able to unravel the infiltration scheme they nearly had solved when the fight became too much for them. However considering the damage done to the pride of their fleet, I expect nothing from them beyond covert reconnaissance for a long time to come. Bellazar is very careful how they invest their assets and traditionally they retreat to study and analyze after a loss. With the Arcadians as their chief nemesis they will spend a lot of time withdrawn into deep speculation. I have no intention of shutting anyone out of the trade situation here; I believe I may have already said that, however I needed a potent show of force to make clear I will not be refused access to a market place. So, at this point are there any questions?" is what Morganti eventually asks.

No one says anything. We soldier girls are in a state of simple shock that the true nature of the situation is being discussed so openly in front of us. Usually we are mushrooms: kept in the dark. I can tell the Major wants to ask something, yet she's keeping herself restrained, so much so that everyone in the room can see and hear her swallowing her words rather than speak. Captain Malloy even rests a hand atop hers.

Morganti addresses the elephant in the Major's throat.

"You want to know the role of Patrice in all of this, why was she here, and what was she doing?" Morganti asks. The question is rhetorical. Morganti doesn't give the Major opportunity to answer. "Patrice does what I want her to do. She takes the assignments I give her, and usually her performance is perfect. Why was she here you want to know? Patrice was here to do something I couldn't ask of you, dear Octavia. Does it hurt you to think I may consider Patrice your equal? Does it outrage you to think I consider her better qualified than you to perform certain tasks? Patrice has little to no aptitude for supervising people, not on any long term basis. Her concept of relationships is... poor at best. That is why she is working alone, and you

Octavia have the soldier girls. Patrice can pilot a starship through the void and the warp possibly better than our dear Jack here, yet I can't trust her to fly a large vessel day in and day out the way we rely on Jack to do so. This is a matter of aptitudes and distinct individual capabilities. I send Patrice to do what she is best at while I send Octavia to do what she is better for, and things get done surprisingly well. I rely on both of you, just in different ways. Although both of you have a surprising propensity and amazing affinity for wet work," Morganti explains, her voice trailing off as she concludes, and her eyes looking downward for a long moment. After the pause she goes on. "Really, I had to say it like that, I mean I've had the two of you kill for me several times, and it's like you both can't get enough. We really need to change the subject," Morganti says when she speaks again. Then she looks about, seeming to evaluate us by eye alone. Then Morganti settles on White and says: "Irwin will actually be here soon to take you all on a real vacation. The soldier girls, not you two," Morganti says, waving a finger at Major Octavia and Captain Malloy. "I want both of you working together on the post-delivery shakedown cruise," she tells them.

Major Octavia doesn't break her professional stone like face when the Widow says this, the Captain, always the more effusive, he just has to ask.

"Post-delivery shakedown cruise? You are aware that turn of phrase implies there is a new ship that needs testing? Quite possibly a new build to put through its paces," Captain Malloy says.

"That's exactly what I'm talking about, Jack," Morganti tells him.

"Hey! What about the soldier boys?" Tiger suddenly demands, jumping to her feet. The outburst is almost completely out of line, yet the question is amazingly valid. Why hasn't anyone asked it yet?

"No one gave you permission to speak," Major Octavia snaps at our sniper.

"The Dowager's Daughter was wrecked in the battle we just fought, and no one has said if they were lost or what. I want to know!" Tiger responds, undaunted by the Major's reprimand. I should have said something, yet the same questions have been hiding in the shadows at the back of my mind as well.

Morganti holds up a hand to silence all. Then she says: "They were offloaded to the *Void Helkein* during your first visit, after you secured this section where we installed the *Janus* command and control system. How do you think we gained full control of this monstrosity? The *Lupus Miles* could only do so much, and while they are intended for ship-to-ship combat, the process was made so much quicker having the soldier boys available. Wait, are you telling me the soldier boys have been absent from the cargo hold of the *Dowager's Daughter* for over a month now and you didn't notice? Who is at fault for that?"

We sit in absolute silence unbroken until Tiger sits back down with her hands in her lap. We ate a big family style supper of squirrel stew in that cargo hold without noticing, didn't we?

"Look," Morganti begins to tell us, and she says: "The soldier boys are intended as medium to heavy infantry, and that makes them well suited to act as security in something like the *Void Helkein*.

They can be deployed anywhere else at any time, just like I do with the *Lupus Miles*. Besides, they won't fit proper in the new ship."

"What new ship?" asks Captain Malloy, sounding anxious and put upon. It will be his toy to make or break.

"They are our family, you could have told us you were taking them away," says White, and she almost gets snapped at just like Tiger did. As it is she only gets a glaring look from the Major.

"Family? Please, I have a daughter, and I work vigorously to avoid the entire situation. I'm hands off there unless forced into it, the family thing. You don't know family until you have had someone you love betray you, cutting your spirit to the deepest level you would think possible or deeper than that even. I mean I've done that so many times I've lost count. I'm the worst, trust me," says Morganti, and then I think she was treating us to her 'evil' laugh. The moment has suddenly turned creepy, or menacing. I need to start being more mature, so the word I will go with is *menacing*.

"Where is this new ship that I suppose you want me to pilot?" Captain Malloy asks.

"I'll get to that, for now I want to talk about something else," Morganti answers him, and for what seems the first time ever she sounds testy, as if weary. I'm guessing she usually doesn't have to endure meetings of this length, not with absolute underlings. She takes a pause, and then with a slight wave, a little gesture of just one hand, she asks the Major and the Captain her question: "So, you two?"

Well, it's not really a question, and while I didn't see it coming, what happens next tells me the

Major and Captain Malloy were ready for it all the time.

"We've talked. We've worked out a lot of issues. This is a real thing," Captain Jack replies.

"So you are no longer available, Jack?" asks Morganti, suddenly looking... what is it, sultry or pouty?

"I don't really have time to date, you know how busy my boss keeps me," Captain Malloy says.

"So if you two are a thing, that means I have one less card to play. I'll have to learn some real management techniques," says Morganti, sounding just as if she's feeling regret, or making the best show of it possible.

This all strikes me as weird, it's as if Morganti is conceding that she has in the past managed both Jack Malloy and Octavia Pomona with deeply visceral emotional manipulation and from what little I have seen in the past, probably some form of extortion. She couldn't have been doing that, could she? Not really? What kind of person could do *that*, and on a *regular* basis? I'm thinking all of this, and realize too late when I have become vocal: "You have a daughter?"

Everyone is silent. The Major is motionless. Captain Malloy is working very intently to stare at a spot on the deck that only he can see. The rest of the soldier girls seem to want an answer to my question as much as I do, yet they are silent as stone, and I didn't even know I was speaking until it was too late.

Morganti is staring at me in a way that makes me want to get up and leave the room. My God, it's like the woman has death-ray eyes. My salvation does not come too soon.

"Mother, it has arrived," an attendant says, standing just at the portal. He's not one of those awful technicians. This is some other kind of fellow who speaks to Morganti, and apparently his words take her mind off of my murder. What was my transgression? I've forgotten. The attendant is wearing the same baggy pajamas as the other one. Who picked out this motif?

"Your surprise is ready," the Widow announces, suddenly full of joy, yet her smile appears to be for Captain Malloy only. Wait, am I wrong in the head, or was it Jack she has given her smile to only? It doesn't matter, because at the moment the Widow is leading us to an observation deck. We hear her ask the attendant: "Is it coming around into view?"

"Yes, Mother. It appears just now," says the attendant, and with a subtle, yet florid gesture of his hand he directs our eyes to the view beyond the window of this observation deck. I keep my eyes on him. How can you be expected to trust a man who wears such a high-collared silk jacket? Does he think it makes him look pretty? Is he trying to appear impressive? He looks like an overdressed menial to me. Like some kind of performing monkey in costume. Then I start thinking about the Chief, and I know I need to find out what became of him... and the deck crew. The Chief never dresses up like some prancing, trained monkey. He's a man. He wears coveralls stained with grease lubricant and smeared with machine oil. That man works for his living. His hands are always dirty. His coveralls are loose, baggy, yet I can still see the cut of his figure. He's caught me watching him. I'm sure about it now. Suddenly my thoughts are brought back to the present when I hear a bunch of sighs and moans of amazement, and when I first try to look out the window I realize everyone is in front of me. Its dark outside, and whatever people are becoming ecstatic about, it is not lit up like a surprise present ought to be. I push my way toward the window and there I see a black diamond floating in the sky. No, actually it is just a delta configured ship, obviously new in every way. Wait, it has wings. Does it have wings? What would you call those things at the aft end, Baffles? I don't know what to tell you. Later I would come to think of them as tail fins. The thing is like a big arrowhead shaped diamond floating in the sky. Presently it's at station keeping just beyond the *Void Helkein*. I have no idea what to make of it, so I begin to look around the room.

"That is no cargo carrier," says Captain Jack, looking at Morganti like she's hatching the most devious secret plot ever conceived.

"I am done with that phase of my plan, dear Jack. I need something more, something better, and you know how often I try to make due with something used. I decided to buy new this time. I found a contractor that promised premium goods delivered at discount prices, and I took them up on the deal. So now you have to test her for me. Jack, I need you to test my *Dowager's Dagger*," Morganti explains to him.

"That's supposed to be our new operational platform? We will need to do more than just test it, Morganti, we will need to learn her, learn who and what she is, and this will not be easy," Captain Jack tells the boss-lady.

"Take all the time you need, only, and just by the way, someone needs to take that admiral's gig thing purloined by Patrice and recover your crew from the surface of Aborto Espontáneo Blanco," says the Widow, with a wave of her hand as if it all is of little importance.

"I've never flown the thing before," says Jack.

"You'll have time to check it out before we go," says Morganti.

"You are going with us to recover the deck apes?" asks Captain Jack.

As he spoke a few of the attendants, all of them in their white silk jackets and pajama pantaloons enter the chamber. They set a tray down upon a table they brought, and lift a silk and linen napkin off the tray. Revealed are a series of large syringes, every one filled with some sort of colorful medicine. At least I presume its medicine. Morganti begins to lightly stroke her hand over each syringe, and then she speaks.

"I'm going down to the planet, Jack. I'm going to seal the deal with that bitch Semiramis," Morganti says, and for some reason I feel a shiver run down my spine.

There is more conversation about what is to be done with the Admiral's Gig. People keep coming back to the notion that if we keep it, if we are found with it, the Arcadians, when they come back, if they come back, will see the Gig, and it will convince them we had a part in the terrible fate that befell their flagship.

Eventually Morganti makes a decision. "Captain Malloy, you and Major Octavia will fly the Gig down to the planet surface, and there it will be abandoned. Any of the settings that you find leave in place. Do nothing that might, on examination, indicate the Gig was in the hands of anyone other than Patrice or the Arcadians who were in possession of the craft. I'm sure she was good about the forensic countermeasures. My own gig will take me and the Soldier Girls down to the planet, and we will find our own way to an audience with Queen Semiramis. My gig will then pick up the two of you and shuttle you to the *Dowager's Dagger*."

"So you want us to set down somewhere like a half-mile away?" asks Captain Malloy.

"At least a mile, and wait for your pick-up," Morganti says, correcting him.

The next day we fly, Captain Malloy and Major Octavia going to ditch the Admiral's Gig and the rest of us with the Widow going to see the Queen. It will be our second attempt, and the last time I think only one of us got to exchange any words with Semiramis. I'm guessing she must be a difficult person. I actually wish I got to see the interior of that Admiral's Gig, to compare it to the accommodations we find in the Widow's private craft. I am telling you this ride is one of the best I've ever had the pleasure to enjoy. The thing is beyond opulent. Not ostentatious, yet it is opulent. Brass framework everywhere, fine wood all over though I think it might be plastic molding, and plush cushions upholstered in the best leather. It's like I'm sitting in someone's lap. Then I realize she is sitting across from me. No one else is in this part of the cabin, they have moved off without my realizing. Where has my head been? Was there a signal that I missed? Why is the Widow sitting here with me, the two of us alone? And Oh My God, why does she have to be looking me straight in the eye?

"Never go near my daughter," Morganti tells me, as she's setting down a black case, setting it down just at her side.

I have no idea what to say. I try to sit still. I try not to show any expression on my face.

"Unless I tell you otherwise, never go near my daughter," Morganti tells me, her arms crossed, her face stern.

I don't say anything. I don't nod, or bob my head, or anything. I have no idea how to react to this, and I have no idea why she is saying any of these things to me. I don't even know the girl's name, or what she might look like, I am sure.

"I had a similar talk with Octavia, and now I need to have it with you. If you hadn't asked, then this conversation wouldn't be happening, yet you did, so here we are, and I know we are both uncomfortable, yet it must be said: stay away from the child, until told otherwise. This command is absolute," Morganti explains.

"Alright," I say, and it is all I say. I know she was trying to be perfectly clear, yet the fact is I am so very confused.

"I'll be putting on some hiking boots in a moment, because we are landing soon and we will be walking, won't we? There's no trollies on this world are there?" Morganti asks.

"Depending on how far we land from where Semiramis holds court we could be in for a very long walk," I tell her.

"I'll trust you to set a perimeter as soon as we touch down?" the Widow says to me.

I nod. I just nod, because the encounter feels that strange to me that I am behaving as if stunned, because I am. I know, if I don't learn how to deal better with the big boss it will kill all my career advancement chances.

Then I watch Morganti raise a hand. She begins snapping her fingers until one of the white pajama boys brings hiking boots for her. I realize the woman is intent on trekking through the jungle in her business suit. Now I desperately hope we are landing close to... well it was a long house where we went to see Semiramis. Not a castle or palace, just a long house. The place was a pretty advanced dwelling for being the construct of primitive people. I mean there was an actual throne room, and other rooms beside that. The place was well maintained, and uncluttered, I know because I was there... I got knocked through a wicker door and then I was brawling on the floor of one room in that long house. Recalling this makes me wonder how warm a reception we might have on the return visit. I mean we were uninvited guests the first time, right? Yet we had those three chiefs with us. I wonder where those guys are now... and if any of them is still looking to get married? Anyway, I get up to rejoin my unit, leaving Morganti to the challenging task of putting on stiff hiking boots with long finger nails. Well, one of her pajama boys is with her, and I see him kneeling to assist as I go.

Chapter Ten

The Widow's gig sets down and the Soldier Girls deploy to establish a perimeter as soon as the hatch opens. I follow my girls out, my scout carbine cradled in my arms, and then I'm shocked to find a hand on one of those arms. First I look at the hand, and then I look at the man that hand belongs to: the Chief of the Boat, the old boat that is gone now: the *Dowager's Daughter*.

"We've been down here for three days, what is up with that?" the Chief asks me, and he must think three days of beard and a big playful smile are attractive because that's just the sort of attitude he's giving off.

"Two days, I'd rather say. I'm not a decision maker around here, you know that," I'm quick to remind the impertinent man. My God, the way he's looking at me. What the hell is wrong with him? Did I miss something? I thought it was the Captain that was collecting his men? I didn't expect to be seeing the Chief. It shouldn't matter, yet I am caught by surprise.

"I doubt I could do better than that pot of stew we enjoyed so much, yet I just have to tell you: I want to try and cook you a meal some time," he says, and I gasp.

I don't know how to react. I'm busy now, why is he pressing me with this... whatever it is? Then the rude jerk lets go of my arm and he's following the rest of the deck apes into the Widow's gig. I stand there slack jawed watching him walk away before I shout out: "You shouldn't complain about how long you were left here! There was a supply of food and water in the life boat good enough for at least three days!"

He turns around and with that infuriating smile of his, he says: "Well I was really complaining about the lack of good company." He seems to gesture toward me then, a casual sweeping gesture of his hand. I have no idea how to respond, and he's gone then inside the gig anyway. I simply stand there for a few moments, my eyes seemingly locked on the hatchway of the gig, and then I hear Green call to me.

"Commander Black? Are you on mission with us? Bad enough we've lost our medic to a man, now our commanding officer?" Green says.

I give her a sour look. This is bad enough without being on the receiving end of ridicule. What makes it even worse is she's teasing me right in front of Morganti, who is looking at me as if making an appraisal. The Widow stands there looking kind of odd in her business suit and hiking boots. Also she carries in one hand that black plastic case I saw earlier. I take Green by the arm and walk her a few paces so we can speak in private. "We need to take special care to look the most professional because of her," I say.

"Yeah, I get you," Green tells me with a nod of her head.

"I should have had this talk with you earlier. We should have done a full mission planning and briefing. Good God, we are boots on the ground in country and we haven't even taken our bearings. Do we know how far we are from the destination site?" I ask.

"Yeah, I worked it out already. I was up toward the cockpit and I talked to the flight crew about the entire navigation situation while you were in the back with the boss-boss," Green replies.

"Boss-boss?" I say, because I just have to ask.

"We are with the *boss of the boss*, you know," Green responds, and does so while giving a very subtle gesture toward the Widow.

"Alright then, so you know where we are going," I say.

"I do. I know you can't be asked to do everything, and without the Major here, that means I have to step up, am I right?" she asks with a smile.

"I'll take point then while you and white flank the VIP fore and aft, and Tiger is our tail. Just point me in the right direction," I say.

"You sure? As long as you say so. I am the one who has been studying the map," Green says, and I still take point anyway, after she gives me a redirect.

We get going in just the moment before the Widow would have lost patience and asked when we would be on our way. I'm glad we get going because I almost never get to walk point. Back in the old days when Tiger and I would be on long range reconnaissance patrol I would be point most of the time, but it doesn't really count when it is just two of you, does it? Tiger usually wasn't point because it was her job to lug around her sniper rifle. Back in those days her weapon system wasn't as big, but it was heavier. Once we are moving the Widow says nothing that I can hear, and I'm sure I would have. I'm not too far out in front, and I never lose sight of the soldier behind me. I receive course corrections from Green periodically, and I follow what she says. There is no one else in the world I trust more. I mean that thing she did where she found out for me our navigation plan? There are people in the world who would have used that against me, and don't believe for an instant they wouldn't. In Green, and all the other Soldier Girls I have friends and colleagues. Another amazing thing? We find our way to the Queen's long house before sunset.

The first reaction of the guards is to point spears at our bellies. These boys are serious. They are tall, strapping muscular men with eyes like ice. I can tell they are ready to kill, and I'm about to say so when another voice fills the air.

"Tell your Queen I am here with the best offer she is going to get," Morganti is telling them as she steps forward.

The cold as ice men on guard duty have a messenger boy. After giving the napping lad a cuff to the head, he wakes; they tell him the message and then dispatch him. I begin to get my head ready to kill natives while we wait. I'm not sure if we wait too long, or if it may have been too quick, I was only sure that things were not going right. Just how they were going wrong I don't know, can't say at all, yet I am sure things are about to go very sideways. Then I think I must be wrong when the boy comes back and only moments after he whispers in the ear of a sergeant of the guard type of fellow we are shown in to see Queen Semiramis.

Of course when we enter the presence of the august queen she is looking just as if she's been in a nasty knife fight. I know, all knife fights are nasty. Yet here we are before Semiramis again, while this time she is bereft of her feather headdress, and most all of her feather finery. What is prominent are her bandages. Semiramis wears more than one poultice. The big on her back is especially noticeable as she isn't sitting upright, more like leaning to one side and protecting the other. When Semiramis looks at us it is like we are sacks of rubbish someone has brought back into the house. Except Tiger, Semiramis looks at Tiger with some strange light in her eyes. I find it inexplicable. If only Tiger knew just home much people like her... then I remember it was Tiger who gave the Queen those wounds.

"You bring these animals back before me?" Queen Semiramis asks of her guards.

"The short one, she said she has something for you my Queen," one of the guards says. I suppose he is Captain, or Sergeant of the guard. It seems strange that he feels at liberty to speak of the Widow of the Market Town as *short*.

"You have a gift to placate my wrath? I have yet to see you kneel before me begging forgiveness," says Semiramis, locking eyes with Morganti. I stand by watching the two most powerful women in the room engage directly.

"I know that if I was to kneel before you, Great Semiramis, then it would only encourage your less gentle impulses," Morganti says in a dead, completely neutral tone of voice. She steps forward moving closer to Semiramis and the throne. "I offer you no gift, Semiramis. What I offer you instead is generous payment for what you know I have been seeking all along," Morganti goes on, while holding up her little black box.

"You want the rocks, the strange rocks that are not meat, not hide or leather, nor feathers to dress your hair or bosom. Why are all of the out worlders so preoccupied with our rocks? You do not throw them at small game when you hunt. From what I gather you don't even hunt most of you. What sort of culture do you come from where merchants and miners are not slaves to the hunting class?" asks Queen Semiramis.

"I am not a hunter, yet I can give you something more valuable than any feathers, leather, or anything a hunter wins in the field. May Semiramis live forever, and I will make it so that she will, if you swear over the rights I seek. If Semiramis gives me what I want, I will give her the most valuable prize I have," Morganti promises the Queen, and then she is opening her special black box, and there we see the syringes she had before, still loaded with whatever chemicals the Widow put inside them.

"I see nothing of value, and why should I give you anything in exchange? Why should I not just take this from you?" asks Semiramis.

"I am the only one here that can administer the treatment, Queen Semiramis, and you need someone knowledgeable or else what I offer will just kill you," Morganti replies.

"You think I cannot endure? You think I am not strong? I am Semiramis! I am Queen! I rule this planet! I rule the three provinces and the most lush hunting grounds in all existence! You think I am not strong enough to endure your poison?" asks the Queen in belligerent defiance.

"I ask you to understand me, wise Queen. I am a ruler and hunter in my own way, and I am here seeking my desired prey. Give me absolute, perpetual rights to your world's mineral wealth, and I will give you immortality, the life of the huntress eternal," Morganti says, and again the two women are locking eyes.

I have got to tell you, they both seem lunatic to me, and I wouldn't be surprised if the savage

Queen Semiramis tried to have her men kill us right here.

"I have made tentative agreements with Bellazar, in exchange for certain things, I have already promised the mineral rights," Queen Semiramis says.

"What have they delivered? I have an initial payment right here. Any others, what have they brought you? Did not Father Drake insert himself among your people as a spy? Was he a spy for you? I understand he spied for Bellazar, and what did he ever do for you?" Morganti asks the Queen.

"Let us do this," Semiramis says, jumping to her feet, and then things became strange... or even stranger I suppose I should say.

"You and you, with me," Morganti says as she points to White and then me in turn. "You two guarantee our privacy," Morganti tells Green and Tiger as we adjourn to a private chamber chosen by Semiramis.

Once secluded Morganti begins to pull some papers from an inside pocket, and she presses the papers and a pen to Semiramis, saying: "Sign here."

Semiramis looks at the papers held out to her, and that's all she does, look with a face twisted by confusion.

Morganti waves the pen, and pointing to the bottom line of one particular page she says: "You put your mark here, giving over to me all the mineral rights of your planet. The strange rocks, you are making them mine, forever. In exchange I promise to make you immortal, like the gods."

Semiramis gives Morganti a bizarre look, and if their eyes locked once again, it was only for a moment. Then Semiramis takes the pen and she makes an elaborate mark upon her signature portion of the page. From what I was able to make out she drew an elaborate animal pictogram, a great cat leaping it seemed. I can't be certain, I only got a glimpse. Morganti looks at the picture on the page for a moment, and then looks at Semiramis.

"It is my crest, my seal. It was created for me at my coming of age ceremony. It incorporates my family name with my birth sign and other aspects of my person. What, is it not good enough?" Semiramis says in response, and she begins to sound indignant there just at the end.

"No, it is perfect," Morganti says, and then looking around, she tells Semiramis: "Now, lie down on the bed."

Semiramis goes to lie down, yet she is ginger slow in her movements. The wound must be painful. Yet her bed is something to see. It appears to be a rather lush bed as compared to any other I have seen on this planet. It is wide enough for three women the size of Semiramis. The room is clearly primitive hunter décor all around. Grim masks hang over the headboard of the Queen's bed, and crossed spears rest there between the masks. Pelts, furs, and other hunter's trophies hang everywhere, confirming everything the queen has said to us about the importance of hunter's culture here on this world.

"Prepare the patient for multiple injections," Morganti tells White, and then looking at me, she says: "Be prepared to assist her in whatever way necessary," as she turns her eyes my way.

"Me, help with injections?" I say, so surprised I don't realize how dumb my question is until the words are already out of my mouth.

"I get it, you are the back-up medic only, and you don't really care for the job. If I had any choice in this matter I would be doing it in a state of the art facility. We don't have that option, so I need you to get on board as a team player, and help prep this patient for a battery of seriously arduous injections. Think you can do that?" Morganti says to me in such a way that makes me feel small and guilty for not *jumping to* the moment she first told me to help. Then she quickly looks back to Semiramis. White has Semiramis by the arm, and is preparing her for the talked about injections, when Morganti says: "No, the liver, I need you to principally sterilize the upper abdomen area so I can give her the injections directly into her liver. That's how this has always been done."

White let's herself show a little frown, and from where she sits on the side of the bed next to where Semiramis lies, White says: "It would help if you let me know what we are doing here first."

Morganti approaches the bed, her black case of syringes held tight, and she sits down on the other side of the bed. Semiramis is looking around suspiciously now. Morganti looks her in the eye, and in a gentle voice I've never heard her use before, Morganti says: "You probably never imagined that I came here already having secured a sample of your individual genetic code, just like your skein as spun by the Fates. That is how invested I am in this operation. I expended the time and resources necessary to gain the key to your very existence and then develop an elixir uniquely keyed to you, dear Semiramis. I have to puncture your form twice, and I am sure you will feel a burning, then pain beyond expectation. I say this because that is how it was for me. Unlike my close research assistant I know this process works best when analgesia is not employed. Also, a curious quirk of your species physiology is a resistance to pain, and a rejection of toxins. It actually turns out you can't benefit from sedatives or pain killers; you are just that hardy a people. So, if we are ready, let's give you immortality."

White has pretty much coated the native woman's upper abdomen with antiseptic, and quicker than a magician can make a coin disappear Morganti is pushing a needle into the spot. I just realized the syringe is all of glass and stainless steel. The glass is thick, and this first injection is of an amber hue. Semiramis is left shuddering and it seems the color fades from her face in an unhealthy way. Well, is there a healthy loss of color for anyone? The moment only gets more tense, more trying from there as Morganti delivers a second injection, and this time it seems like she is squirting actual mercury into the belly of Semiramis. Good God, what have I become a part of?

"Be ready to run," Morganti suddenly says.

"What?" I have to ask.

"This has only been done three times in the past. I've never done this to another person. I've only done this to myself. I was getting the best possible help then on top of that. So I have no idea what will happen this time. As I said: be ready to run," Morganti explains. Her explanation leaves more questions than it offers answers.

"She could die?" I ask, actively dropping my voice as much as I can and still be heard.

"Yes," Morganti answers, looking at me as if I'm an idiot. Well, if she can make a working eternal youth potion, then yes, compared to her I am an idiot. Except if we do need to run away, I'll be the idiot keeping her alive.

"It appears our patient has slipped into a coma. Was that anticipated?" White asks, sounding very professional, yet very concerned.

"Normally the patient would be sedated, or in an induced coma. When I examined what is known about the people of this world, and when I read this woman's genetic code, I knew sedation was precluded. If she is comatose, and quickly comes out of it on her own, then all will be well. If she is in a coma as a prelude to death, that is bad," Morganti explains.

"We may have just killed the queen of the world?" White asks, and her concern is now mingled with unease.

"Just this world," a blasé Morganti says in reply. Then she continues: "Eight to twelve hours, that's usually all it takes for the formula to do its work, and for the subject to come out of it. When they are recovered from the injections they usually feel better than they ever have in their lives. I slept for twelve hours when I took the injections. The second subject was out for sixteen. The third subject was unconscious overnight, from what I hear. I wasn't a part of that procedure. Not a willing part I should say. Quite a larcenous band of monsters they were who perpetrated that iteration of my prize research."

"Your research?" asks White.

Morganti smiles in a way that I am sure most of the time is taken to be endearing, quite charming, yet at the moment I can only feel anxiety.

Thinking about what Morganti just said, I have to press her with a question: "You mentioned three other times this has been done, and this is only the first time you have done it with a blue skinned alien. So you don't really know what to expect, do you?"

"I read her genetic code, so I knew exactly how to modify my *Life Extension* formula," Morganti says, giving me a testy look.

"*Your formula*? As in those injections were a thing of your creation?" I ask, genuinely surprised.

"My creation in a previous life, because I'm a business woman now, not a genetic engineer," says Morganti, with a quality of weariness entering her voice.

"You used to be a genetic engineer?" White asks, sounding professional, even clinical.

"I studied genetic engineering, when I was working toward my doctorate. It was all a very long time ago, and there are no ghosts remaining from that era... or they should all be gone... it doesn't matter!" Morganti insists, and she has a sudden need to shut her eyes tight and massage her temples.

"She's a doctor?" White whispers to me.

Morganti doesn't seem to hear the question, and even if I could answer, I don't get the chance, because someone knocks at the door. It opens enough for Green to lean her head inside. She wants to tell me something so I go over to listen.

"The guards are acting oddly. I'm suspicious," Green tells me.

"You think they are about to make a move?" I ask.

"I think they are definitely working up the nerve," Green replies.

"Keep us posted," I tell her, and then I turn back to Morganti and I cast a glance toward the sleeping Queen. I want to say her color is returning. I can't be certain about that, too much possibility its just wishful thinking.

"Are we going to have trouble?" Morganti asks.

"The pot is on the stove," I reply.

"What?" Morganti asks, expressing her confusion.

"It's cooking, or brewing, yes, we may be facing trouble. Don't get fretful, not yet. I have two of the best at the door, and that's enough to assuage my fears," I tell her, and did you catch that? I said *assuage*, now you know I can use big words too, when the spirit is upon me.

Morganti shows me her frown. She looks at me hard from under her brow, crossing her arms, and I think I may have gone too far. It is probably just the situation. Here we are in an alien landscape, and among an alien people. We have possibly killed their Queen, and God only knows what is going to happen. A dead Queen won't make it any better, and that I can assure you. I turn my attention to the sleeping Queen, and my unit medic to see how things look. I'm about to ask White for a situation report when Morganti speaks up afore me.

"Are you watching her vitals?" the Widow asks.

"I am, and it seems her pulse and heart rate are racing, unless this is just the resting norm for her species?" White responds.

"Their nominal metabolic rate is much more rapid that ours. They are big meat eaters, lots of fat and protein in their diets, and no refined sugars. That's why on average they seem to be so much longer and leaner than we," Morganti explains.

"What, no dairy in their diets?" I ask. While I say it as if a jest, I'm actually curious.

"You've been spending time here, did you see any cows, goats or anything that men keep that gives milk?" Morganti asks.

I nod, and then I begin to think about her comment about the people of this world being longer and leaner. Honestly, to me Semiramis seems only slightly taller and leaner than I or the other soldier girls. Then I recall how diminutive the Widow is compared to us. Also I quietly reprimand myself for not easily recalling to what extent dairy is part of these people's diet. Well, I was exposed mostly to the hunting class, the dominant class of the culture here as they represent it. I know there are farmers and other producers of consumables. I mean there just has to be fishermen, yeah? Yet the people we have dealt with and all the folks we have seen, the hunters have been the most prominent, and powerful. Then the door to the Queen's room opens and it is Green holding the door while Tiger comes inside. "What's happening?" I ask, watching Green shut the door quickly after Tiger who is dashing to the far side of the bed to set up her weapon system. "Oh crap," I say, watching Tiger deploy the bipod legs of her rifle, and lay it across the bed, over the top of the Queen's shin bones.

"What is happening?" asks Morganti.

As I'm trying to think of a good way to put it, Tiger says it, and probably better than I would have.

"Stage two of pre-engagement escalation, ma'am," Tiger tells the Widow as she looks down the sight of her rifle.

Morganti is now looking to me for confirmation, or explanation. She wants to know something.

"My people think things are about to get ugly, really very ugly, and I have no reason to doubt or second guess them. For now I'm going outside to take a look and talk to my Lieutenant," I tell Morganti, and then I turn away, doing what I said.

Stepping through the door, and to one side, I look at Green, and then I look around. People are moving around as if they don't want anyone to notice them. They are acting as if everything is normal. I can see how cagey they are, how wound-up they've become and they're trying to hide it. Green and I meet eye to eye for a moment, and I can tell she has been thinking just what I am now. These people are putting on an act. They want us to believe they aren't up to something. We pick up on this because they don't seem busy. They just seem tense, on edge. Normal people in normal situations can often move about as if it is critical they handle whatever is on their mind. An example: *'If I don't get these packages to the mail room right now, then I am dead!'* Silly garbage like that, it over takes people's mindsets. This is especially so of the staff in a place like a Queen's residence. The environment is normally dripping with artificially generated nervous energy. This is why I am glad I have spent so much of my lifetime away from such environments. Now I stand at a doorway, looking to see what trouble may be coming up, and I know things are going to turn bad very soon. No telling when, just soon.

When I realize the moments of observation have now passed I look at Green and I tell her: "Be ready to make a hot egress."

"I see the pot about to boil," Green responds.

'Thank God we are on the same page,' I think as I go back into the room. Once inside, and with the door closed behind, I issue an instruction in my clearest command voice: "We need to make a bolt hole."

****

Queen Semiramis has a council, her *Queen's Men* so to speak, and they are of two minds. Half the Queen's Council wants a king, or a regent, or something other than Semiramis. She really is that unpopular with some of the people. The other half wants to know what is happening to their Queen, and they don't care what off-worlder they have to kill to find out. Both wings of the Queen's Council can agree that they will have to send warriors into the Queen's chamber with orders to secure the Queen, and bring her out, alive or dead. There is a Grand Vizier raving for armed men to be sent into the Queen's chamber, and while he is careful how he is choosing his words, everyone knows the Grand Vizier covets the Queen's seat. There is a High Chancellor who wants the Queen's guards to confront the Off-Worlders, demanding to see the Queen and know her condition. While he bears Semiramis no ill-will, he really doesn't care if the Queen should be killed in the course of a melee with outsiders. There is a wealthy Satrap who makes a big show of expressing concern for the Queen and her welfare, yet everyone knows he styles himself the heir to Semiramis, and that means if she dies, no matter how, he sees himself acceding to the throne. The odd thing is in spite of the abundant titles Semiramis has given these men of her council, in the eyes of the people of their world they are really nothing more than overdressed chiefs. Since most of the councilmen do not have any actual landholdings they are chiefs in name only, at least in the eyes of the people. For her heavy handed ways Semiramis may be an unpopular Queen. Yet she is their Queen, and a successful huntress nearly beyond compare. The Chiefs may tend to be old, fat, lazy and greedy, yet they are all men who earned their place in society by their success in the hunt. The Councilmen, while they may have been good hunters at one time, or at least each one of them had a good day on the hunt at some time in the past, they are not hunters anymore. Now the Council men are politicians in a society that worships the hunter and his exploits. They hunted at one time, and they can still remember what it is to kill. Now they speak of killing once again and in the shadows a watcher is biding time, waiting for the opportune moment to act.

Captain Jack executed a perfect landing of the purloined Admiral's gig with Major Octavia in the co-pilot seat. He turned his head, saying to her: "We rendezvous with the deck apes, and the Widow's gig flies us to our new ship."

"No," responds Major Octavia.

"What are we doing then?" Captain Jack asks.

"You will be gathered to your men, and go to the new ship. I am paid to protect Morganti, not give some new toy a shake-down," Major Octavia says, checking all of her gear as she speaks. Octavia doesn't even spare a moment to meet his eye.

"She told us both to go the new ship," says Jack.

"I'm not necessarily paid to do what I am told, Jack. I am surely paid to do monstrous things and to be a monster. That is what Morganti needs. I know my job, Jack, and you better not get in the way of my doing it," Octavia tells him, and now she is looking him in the eye. He would rather she hadn't, not like this. He wasn't about to object further, yet the look in her eye was so unnerving. It was one of the few moments she *wasn't* wearing her dark glasses. Now Octavia pulls her heavy black trench coat around her shoulders, goes out the door and out into the Jungle on her own.

Semiramis wakes with a start, and I mean she really wakes with sudden and powerful excitation. She gasps as she sits straight up in her bed. Her eyes are wide open, although they seem like dark slits of gleaming evil to me. I didn't say that before, did I? Anyway, her breathing is rapid, and she looks quite tense.

"You should lie back down and let me check your vitals," says White as she reaches out to the Queen, trying to gently push the woman back down to the mattress. Of course Semiramis pushes her off and not so gently.

"I am Queen, not some child to be put to bed by a nurse!" barks Semiramis.

"I have to make sure you are not having an adverse reaction, that your condition is good," White says.

"I have been in worse condition and issued death sentences," says Semiramis. No one questions what she means by that statement, I mean really, do you think we want to listen to any story this lady has to tell?

"Let her check you out," Morganti tells the Queen, and the command takes hold.

Semiramis lies back, and White puts a stethoscope to her breast.

"What is she doing?" demands Semiramis, pointing at Tiger who still rests her sniper rifle across the Queen's legs.

"Standing ready to protect you if need be. Now be quiet and let the girl check your heart and pulse," says Morganti.

Why do I get the feeling Morganti and Semiramis don't see an equal when they look around most any room? Then I notice the way Semiramis is moving one of her hands. It's like she's stroking Tiger by the hair, yet her arm isn't long enough to reach Tiger's head all the way down at the far end of the bed.

"What are you doing now?" demands Morganti.

"I wish I could stroke her hair for real, she is the only one to ever subdue me in a tussle. You have to admire that in another," Semiramis says of Tiger who now looks a tad uncomfortable.

This is when Green suddenly jumps back into the room, shutting the door behind her, slamming it hard. I don't know why but she stands to the side in a peculiar way after slamming the door shut. Then I see the spear tips punch through wood. "They want to kill her!" Green says, looking at me with fear in her eyes.

Chapter Eleven

"Open the bolt-hole now!" I scream, flipping the selector switch of the carbine to full automatic and I put the stock to my shoulder. I fire where I think the spearmen will be, and watch my bullets tear through old wood. Then I look to see what is happening on the other side of the room. Tiger is using her knife to cut a hole in the wicker wall. White is trying to keep out of the sniper's way. Morganti looks to be quite on edge, yet she is letting her professional staff do their jobs. She deserves a lot of credit for not getting in our way at the moment. Semiramis is still very agitated.

"What is happening?" she demands.

"Palace revolt," says Green as she takes Semiramis by the arm, pulls her off the bed, and guides her over to stand beside Morganti. Getting the luminaries out of the way, that was a good idea on her part. Then I see Green begin to pull at the headboard of the bed, and I figure out what she has in mind. I help her push the bed against the door. "They are only regrouping, I'm sure of it. The only question is how much time will they need?" Green asks me.

"Depends on how many I hit and killed," I say, and then looking at Semiramis, I ask: "How often do your guards face gunfire?"

"This generation has never faced weapons like yours," she tells me, very direct, and matter of fact.

"You really mean never?" I ask, her response taking me by surprise.

"They have seen weapons like yours before, yet they have never faced such weapons until these most recent visitations by outsiders," Semiramis explains, and I recall the gunfire that erupted just before our first planned visit.

I check what progress Tiger has made, and a hole in the wall big enough to jump through is what I see. Then more spear tips are punching through the door. "We got to get out of here," I say, and then it is axe heads they start in with and it is even more obvious that door won't last. "Tiger and White: take point, Semiramis and Morganti you two go next and then Green and I will cover our tail," I order and while Green has her eyes locked on the disintegrating door, I watch my girls climb through the hole. Then something curious happens: Semiramis leaps through like an acrobat and Morganti having watched Semiramis, she mimics the action.

"Now you go," I tell Green, and then she is climbing through the hole. Some other time we will have to figure out why Semiramis and Morganti are so much more agile and coordinated than are my Soldier Girls. Now I have to send a message to the insubordinate praetorians. Stock to shoulder again and I fire my weapon until the magazine runs dry. I have made the door a ruin, yet the men who were trying so hard to get through it, they have a new set of quite dire problems, if they are still alive.

This is when I turn, make as quick a leap through the bolt hole as I can, and then struggle to get my leg loose from the snag that holds me in place. I'm left hopping on one foot, the splintered wall refusing to let go the hold it has on my pant leg.

"Come on," Green is hissing at me from the shadows.

I get my leg free and then I am chasing after my command. I have to get us all out of this alive, my Soldier Girls, our employer, and our employer's very special guest.

The watcher had climbed to the top of the Queen's long house, and from there planted four small yet powerful incendiary devices in anticipation of what was to come. The watcher knew havoc was about to erupt any moment, she only needed to wait. Then there was a second burst of gunfire followed by the sight of six figures running off into woods. This is when the watcher detonated her fire bombs, actually thin strips of plastic explosive that set ablaze the crude shingles of the longhouse roof. Then the watcher puts her boot to a weak spot in the roof punching a hole and she let herself drop inside.

Landing on her toes, Octavia draws her knife, a long and sleek dagger with a needle sharp deadly point. She comes up behind one warrior and has drawn her blade across his throat faster than his thoughts realized she was there. A second warrior gets stabbed twice in the kidney and he cries out something horrible, yet Octavia is in the shadows before anyone can see her. When next she appears Octavia knocks aside a spear with her tactical baton and slashes her second throat. The man isn't dead when he hits the floor, yet he will be soon. The whisper thin blade cuts that deep. Then Octavia is spinning out of the way of a spear attack, blocking with her baton again, and when she comes out of the spin she slashes another man to his death. Amazingly only the barest splatter of blood stains Octavia, even after cutting down four men.

Commander Black had cut down at least a dozen men with her bursts of carbine fire, and Major

Octavia has easily cut down four men with her diversionary attack. Major Octavia means to stall pursuit of Morganti and Semiramis, there are still at least a hundred men all set on capturing or killing the Queen and the off-world interlopers. This forces Major Octavia into a different posture. She must escape, and she must do so following a path that will not lead any who follow her to the Queen or the Widow that Octavia serves.

****

"My brother will be avenged," the Colonel says.

On board the Arcadian Flagship *Iowa* the executive officer of the Admiral's staff is fuming, positively fuming. Indeed, he could barely contain himself.

"If our sister ship is not here, then someone better tell me where it is, and now!" the officer demands of the crew.

"The *Kiowa* is due to arrive any moment, Colonel Brackenbok," calls out a young woman working at an operations station.

"My brother will be avenged," the Colonel is barely heard, as he tries to keep his voice down this time. Yet his muttering draws attention.

"Pardon, Colonel?" asks the girl from the operations station.

"Never mind him, I want a status report," a voice calls out.

"Attention on deck!" Colonel Brackenbok shouts out at first sight of the speaker.

"As you were, I need my status report, not vain formalities," says the speaker having entered the bridge. She wears the stylized jumper of a navy sailor, similar to what a school girl would wear, complete with scarf, back flap and a pleated skirt.

"Princess Armida, we are still waiting for the task force to assemble. *Kiowa* is inbound, and *Iroquois* is at standby," says Colonel Brackenbok delivering the report. He stands perfectly ramrod straight in his stiff army uniform. The collar alone should be killing him.

"The squadron will consist of three ships, is that all? I was told something of twenty would be the number," Princess Armida replies, and with a sigh she says: "This is supposed to be a reprisal mission of ultimate sanction."

"Time constraints trump big talk about overwhelming force, Princess," Colonel Brackenbok states.

Armida looks at him with sympathy, and in a quiet tone she asks: "Are you sure you should be on this mission, Colonel? You just lost a sibling. Your judgement and objectivity could possibly be clouded?"

"I am under orders to join this task force, Princess Armida," the Colonel says.

"Orders that may have been written in your own hand, and then signed by a crony in the admiralty," Armida comments, still speaking low under her breath.

Colonel Brackenbok is very quiet, and very still.

"We have served together my entire career, Colonel. While this is a mission of reprisal, it is not for your personal revenge," Armida tells the man.

"My brother is dead, to what extent do you expect me to set aside emotion?" the Colonel demands. He has not raised his voice, and though he speaks in low tones, the angry rasp in his voice is unmistakable.

"To the extent necessary that you can still perform your duties, Colonel, and if I must, I will scrub you from the mission. I'll have you shoved into an evacuation suit and tossed out an airlock if I have to because this is the largest, most important mission I've ever been given the privilege to command," Armida explains to the Colonel.

"Princess, you are aware..." begins the Colonel, yet his voice trails off.

"Colonel, what is it?"

"There is another..." he says with his voice trailing off again.

"Just spit it out man," demands Armida.

"Your sister is on board, and you know how she is about your authority," the Colonel finally tells her.

"Dear God, they sent the monster along? Will she ever plague me?" asks Armida.

"And her cohort," adds Colonel Brackenbok.

Armida simply sighs. Then she closes her eyes, drops her head for a long moment of self-pity. "Of course, where my sister goes her mad *Einsatzgruppen* follows.

"*Kiowa* and *Iroquois* are falling into formation," announces the crew member working the communications station.

"So we have our three ships, and we are ready to go, though seventeen fewer than I was promised, yet this should be good enough," Armida comments, affecting a kind of blasé resignation.

"Battleship *Alabama* reports ready to jump," calls out that same crewmember from the communications station.

"Your pardon, where is the *Alabama*?" Armida is forced to ask.

"*Alabama* is on station at the transition point," the girl from the operations station replies.

"Well then, four ships," Armida says.

"We are still waiting for the Admiral, my Princess," Colonel Brackenbok tries to remind Armida.

"I am here, Colonel," Armida says.

"You are not an Admiral," says Colonel Brackenbok.

"No, I am a Princess, and a Princess always outranks an Admiral, always!" shouts Armida, nearly hysterical it seems as she clenches her fists, and thrusts them down by her sides, while stomping a foot.

"Our orders, Princess," says Colonel Brackenbok.

"I have friends in the Admiralty as well, Colonel, and I can assure you as well as show you that I am the officer in overall command of this task force and its mission," declares Armida.

While Colonel Brackenbok had full faith in the Princess, he couldn't help but think they would be better off with an experienced, cool headed Admiral in their company.

****

"My brother will be avenged!" screams Admiral Mallakastra Malebranche as she walks onto the bridge of her flagship, the dreadnought *Red Unicorn*. Her eyes dart about quickly seeking any sign of defiance.

Every sailor present jumps to attention, and waits. Every one of them is terrified of incurring the

Admiral's wrath. Obviously she's already in an over-heated condition. The Admiral simply stands there for several moments, glaring at the crewmen. Then she shouts: "All stations report!"

"All stations report ready. The *Red Unicorn* is able to depart on your word, Admiral," responds a sailor.

"We have three ships in our squadron, I want to know their status, now!" howls the incensed Admiral.

"*Black Unicorn* reports ready for your orders, Admiral," reports that same crewmember.

"And our third?" asks the Admiral, her eye glaring down at the sailors.

"*Silver Unicorn* reports last checks for getting underway in progress," says another crewmember.

"Why is *Silver Unicorn* always late?" demands Admiral Mallakastra, striking her fist upon a hand rail.

'*How did an immature psychopath like you become a flag officer?*' some stray crewmember is thinking.

"*Silver Unicorn* is within schedule parameters," an officer says to the Admiral. He's the highest ranking officer on the bridge, other than the Admiral, and actually he's the commanding officer of the *Red Unicorn*, so by technicality he should be safe saying this to the Admiral. Also, Captain Charles Dalmatian has a rather distinguished career record speaking volumes about his competence; otherwise he wouldn't have been given a prestigious assignment like command of the *Red Unicorn*.

"My brother has been humiliated by the Arcadians, all Belazar has been humiliated, and you speak to me of schedules? You dare?" growls the Admiral at Captain Dalmatian with eyes full of hate.

The Captain of the *Red Unicorn* nearly falls to temptation, and yet the moment before he would have spouted his worst insubordination is when the communications officer announces the *Silver Unicorn* is reporting ready to get underway.

"Then make it happen! Squadron *Unicorn* underway! We make for the warp-rift at top speed! And if those soft bodies on the *Silver Unicorn* are tired, or just not feeling quite right, then tell them their flag officer is still legally permitted to punish by flogging!" shouts Admiral Mallakastra.

****

We ran hard through the night, and those first hours we were running all the harder for having seen the fire bomb that surely destroyed the long house from where Queen Semiramis had ruled her nation. When she saw the explosion and all the flames, Semiramis was given pause.

"*Lupus Formosus* now lives here," she said, tapping her breast. She stood so tall, so straight, and looked so dignified that for a moment I almost forgot how awfully she spoke to us most of the time. Mind you, for a nearly naked savage, she is fantastically beautiful. I have to wonder if she felt exposed without all her feathers and other finery.

"*Lupus Formosus*, that's an interesting name. Not of the native tongue, is it?" asks Morganti.

"The first missionary who came here, Father Gentle, that is what he called this world. In our own tongue this world is simply called *the world*. We have no special name for it, yet Father Gentle admired our ability as hunters, as all should. He said we hunt like wolves, and he thought of the people here as being so beautiful. I found that strange because it is known that until the day of his death he never took even one female, not even those who approached him," replies Queen Semiramis.

"That's because he must have been a true missionary, and not a fraud like Drake," Green says, and I let the moment of impertinence slide, although I shouldn't.

Semiramis regards Green for a moment, and then turns her attention elsewhere. She looks from Morganti to me, and if trying to decide who to address. A moment passes in silence and I am about to speak up because I know we can't just stand around. There are surely people, armed men, in pursuit of us. Then Semiramis speaks: "You are the Chieftain of this hunting party," she says pointing to Morganti, and then she looks Tiger: "While you are the true huntress," and then she turns to me, saying: "While you are the leader of this hunt."

"You have a good approximation of the facts," I tell the Queen.

"We have to travel North West, the tribes in that direction will be most sympathetic to my dilemma," Semiramis tells me, as she points in an actual north westerly direction.

"Right, I'll take point, Tiger trails me, then White, and Green you cover our rear," I order, and then we are moving again with the dawn appearing behind us. We make good time, and I'm amazed because I never thought the luminaries would be able to keep up. While Semiramis is a local, and so she's covered ground like this all her life, she's also the Queen, and has been sedentary in her role as ruler. I can't be sure of her capabilities because I don't really know her, and I certainly know very little about her species. Yet Morganti is the real puzzle because as far as I know she's just a woman, right? She's very youthful in her appearance; she can't be more than twenty I would think unless I judge her wrong. The way she moves reminds me of someone we met once long ago, even before we went to prison. I think about that while we make good time and the walk is comfortable with the sun mostly at our backs and some breeze in our face.

We are hard at it, walking through the morning, and only the quickest stops for water. Never dehydrate, never. Yet for all the good time we make I begin to get the feeling there are eyes upon us. I can't fault the feeling, we are in a jungle. Rule of the jungle is there are always eyes upon you, and you can be sure at least one set of those eyes belongs to a predator. The feeling actually grows, and I begin to look over my shoulder. Tiger is nearby following me in the order of march and the third time I look backward she says: "More than one."

I hold my fist up right then and there signaling for a stop. Tiger takes two steps closer to me and she says: "I know what you are worried about, and I have to tell you I think it's more than one."

"Well yeah, it's a jungle, there has to be more than one critter out there looking at us," I reply.

"No, I mean it isn't just the critters, there is something else with eyes on us, they just know how to go unseen. They are good, real good, and they might be stalking us outright," Tiger says.

"How much time you think we got?" I ask.

"At the distance they are keeping? I don't think they plan to make a move on us, not yet," Tiger answers.

"Then we keep moving I have to suppose," but I walk back down the line to where Semiramis stands, Morganti nearby, just behind her. "How long do you think until we reach your friendly village?"

"Midday, I am sure we can reach the village of the *Dine'e* by midday," Semiramis pronounces with confidence.

White make an odd sound, probably distress and I recall the *Dine'e* Chief made it known to the girl just how friendly he could be. "Any candy left in those pockets?" I ask walking by her as I go on point once again, and then I say: "Come on then, we should try to make it to the *Dine'e* village in time for luncheon." And then we are marching once more.

It might be closer to one in the afternoon when we reach the *Dine'e* village, yet I can't be certain because honestly I have no idea how close or far this planet varies from the normal twenty-four hour day. We have been calling this world *Aborto Espontáneo Blanco*, an appellation meant to be derogatory, and have only just recently learned the ruler prefers to call her world *Lupus Formosus*. Strange it seems what details have fallen to the wayside in our effort to secure *mineral rights*. Walking into the village under the mid-day sun is different this time, and not just because we arrive at a different time of day. This time we walk into the midst of the *Dine'e* with their Queen and Empress at our side. A lot of eyes open big and wide. Jaws drop and so many villagers are whispering that it becomes like a roar in our ears. The really interesting thing is that once we are within the village Queen Semiramis leaves us in her wake. She goes straight to the village chief, the headman, to speak directly.

"I need your hospitality, at least for one night. Will you help your Queen? I have become vexed by fools. Will you help your Queen? I will soon have to hunt brothers who have forsaken our family. Will you help your Queen?" Semiramis says to the man.

"I will give you respite, at least for one night, yes I will help my Queen. I will stand beside you if fools should come to do you harm, yes I will help my Queen. If family betrays family, then yes I will help my Queen," responds the Chief of the *Dine'e*.

At the moment I'm sure I've just witnessed a ritual exchange.

Semiramis turns to us, and she says: "We will rest here, take food, and with the dawn some men will join us to visit the *Dunne-Za*."

Except that isn't what happened, and I assure you I would have preferred to follow the Queen's plan to the letter, yet we were forced to do otherwise. The *Dine'e* fed us shortly after we arrived, and again that evening. After running all night and half the day getting to eat well and relax was of great benefit. And I have told you how these people fire roast just the freshest meat you will ever taste, right? This time the carcass was stuffed with some kind of roots or tubers, much like garlic and onion, and though they did this only because they were entertaining the Queen, I'm not complaining. I mean we had gone eighteen hours without anything more substantial than the smallest portions of field rations, and while that's no big problem for my Soldier Girls, I thought it would be very hard on the luminaries. Except, Semiramis and Morganti didn't complain much at all. They seemed unusually vibrant, especially after the lunch. Actually Semiramis never complained, and it stemmed from the days of her youth when she proved herself a huntress. She tells us stories that night of how she was sent out into the jungle as an adolescent with only spear and hunting knife. This is a traditional story I have heard in the past, and during my training days I experienced something similar, except in my case and most others the youthful initiate is given something else, like a sack of dry cereal such as oats or something of the like. Also Semiramis specified she was sent out naked, just a leather thong tied around her midriff, barely a string of animal hide used only to hang her knife sheath. This must be a very common story because all the people of the *Dine'e* gathered and listening were nodding their heads knowingly, as with approval, as if they had all been through it themselves. Except they hadn't, and while I've made it clear that hunting dominates the culture of this world, Chiefs and Royals, such as Semiramis, they perform this ritual hunting trip alone, and for an extended period, much longer than anyone else who endures the rite of passage. Also because some holy man, a shaman, or something of the like had singled out Semiramis as a likely ruler someday, she was left alone for so very long a time in one of the most isolated and dangerous of the wild territories. Semiramis had to do her test in a section of jungle more like Gehenna than any place I have ever seen. At least, the way she tells the story I become convinced of it. That part of the evening was actually very enjoyable. Hearing her stories of her youth left me feeling a new found bond with Semiramis. If she had a hard exterior and difficult attitude, at least now I had some sense about it. The problem was that the whole night wasn't just story telling. There were noises, and not the sort of sounds the *Dine'e* knew so as to take comfort. No, the strange sounds the were being heard from the jungle, clearly coming from the east were frightening, and it showed, even in the eyes of the locals, maybe even more so. Eventually I had to ask.

"What is this? Why do you shudder at those sounds?" I demand of a woman sitting nearby.

"The Destroyers, the sound of the Destroyers is what we hear now," she tells me, her eyes filled with terror.

I turn away from the woman, taking her to be an obvious idiot. We barely know anyone here, having visited this place only once before and so very briefly. I decide a minimum of action needs to be implemented. "Team, key on our Luminaries," I say, and this brings the Soldier Girls to their feet. We need to collect Morganti and Semiramis, and try to form a defensive perimeter. The *Dine'e*, they are more than just restless by now, they are getting up, making their way for the western exit. I look to the east. Nothing is coming through the doors, yet the awful sounds, shrieks and screams, persist. I look back to the luminaries, and Semiramis meets me by the eye.

"We should leave, after the others are gone," she tells me.

"What is really going on here?" I demand to know from Semiramis.

"She told you, that woman said: '*the destroyers*' or did you not hear?" replies Semiramis in that tone of hers that reminds me why some people hate her.

"Why aren't you afraid?" I ask.

"This is not the time! You need to get us out of here," snaps Morganti.

"Well the others have pretty much cleared out. So let's begin our own egress," I say, and we begin to turn toward the western door. You just have to know the situation was worse the way we went.

Every single one of the villagers was gone, yet something was there, waiting for us. They were tall, nearly giants, and they were coming in through that western door like victors. A quick look back showed others that were identical were coming in through the eastern door. I began to understand how they had been nearly invisible in the jungle, and now the night. They were standing there naked and their skin was black. They were almost as dark as the night itself. Yet their hair and eyes were red, just like fresh blood. These were monsters I tell you and something I never would have imagined real, yet they are here now right before us. They were even more alien than I have yet told you. Each one that now stood just as if confronting us had six arms and six breasts. Good God, are they supposed to be female? They hold long spears that shine like silver, and their fingers have long nails that gleam, just as if silver as well. Every moment before these monstrosities was worse than the last because it was after we took in all of these details a few of them parted their lips, bearing fangs, silver fangs that made me feel like I was about to become supper for a super natural monster. One of them came forward, and she was distinguished from the others by a silver belly chain she wore. I also noticed her silver spear was longer, and had enhancements the other didn't possess. As shocking as all this was, what happened next nearly too much.

Semiramis stepped forward, she walked up to the one I would learn to be the leader, and the Queen spoke, bravely, and with a steady voice, she said: "This is my time, to be judged before I go to the afterworld, yes? I am not afraid."

The monster sneered, an ugly sight with her mouth full of metallic fangs, and she grabbed hold of Semiramis to toss her aside. One of the others caught Semiramis and threw her away even further. The Queen hit the floor, hard, and then another of the monsters was forcing her back to her feet, and held her there. The leader stepped closer, she moved toward Morganti, and I was worried how horrid the scene would be if a fight broke out. The leader bent at the hip, lowered her head toward Morganti, and sniffed deep a few times. She seemed to point at Morganti as if confirming something to the others, and then I'm not sure what happened.

Chapter Twelve

Octavia had been running, hiding, and fighting for the equivalent of a day and a half, at the least. The whole time the Soldier Girls were escorting Morganti and Semiramis to the *Dine'e* village, Octavia was in the jungle fighting to slow down those men of power who wanted to do their Queen harm. Many wanted to depose her, some even wanted to kill Semiramis. She was slowing them down every way she could. Trip wires, some rigged to booby traps, some just wires strung tight across trails, Octavia had alternated these traps. At least four times she had jumped out of the woods and slashed a man's throat, usually a straggler. These attacks were very demanding on her stamina because they had to be set up in advance, and then she was forced to run like mad when the other men realized she had killed one of their number. It was also unpleasantly messy because no matter how skilled Octavia was at that sort of blitz attack, she would inevitably get blood on her hands, it's nearly impossible not to when you are cutting throats.

After winnowing their numbers Octavia began the drag effect, or crippling attacks. Again she would emerge from concealment as fast as she could, yet now she would stab to wound. A well placed jab to the kidney, or better, the lung, and the enemy was left with an ally who needed care, slowing down all else they sought to achieve. Octavia got one man in the kidney, and he went down screaming. While they all stood over him in concern Octavia was able to sneak around them again, and this time she jabbed her knife under a man's ribs, making a deep cut in his right lung. The pursuers were about as on edge as they could be, two men were down, and they were being forced to split their numbers. It would take two men to help one wounded man head back to the village, the same place with the burned remains of the Queen's long house. Just as they were getting that whole effort underway they became victim of another blitz attack. Octavia darted in, diving low to stab a man at the inner thigh. She managed to slice him deep, and the cut was long. He went down screaming, and his blood was flowing free. The others tried to help him, yet a cut like that to a major artery is a death sentence, and that's just what happened. By now all these men who thought to kill Semiramis, they were angry, frightened, and suffering profound confusion about what to do next. This is how Octavia kept them from getting anywhere near their Queen, even though Octavia was principally thinking about the safety of Morganti. Little did Octavia know the real problem came with nightfall.

The high ranking men gave up hope as their numbers were cut and Octavia went on tracking the Soldier Girls and the luminaries to the village of the *Dine'e*. It was as she tracked her people that Octavia realized others were involved, and it vexed her because she tried to spot them, tried to find sign of them, and couldn't. Octavia only had a feeling something or someone was out there in the jungle and she could do nothing. Octavia would stop and listen, yet it didn't matter how still she was. It didn't matter how hard she looked out into the jungle, or up into the canopy, and remember Octavia has her glasses, her special glasses. Standing motionless, like statuary, Octavia would adjust her glasses, looking through the entire spectrum of luminal wavelength, various bands of radiation, trying even for just a glimpse. The feeling Octavia has that something is out there, she finds it inescapable, the sense of it absolutely immutable. Yet what she seeks is able to avoid all detection. It was as if something, whatever it was, that it's capable of avoiding detection until it wants to be seen. Octavia has never faced anything like this before. Usually she is the one hidden from all sight. Octavia pushes on, heading to the *Dine'e* village. She has no other choice.

It was in the night when Octavia first saw them, and perhaps it can be called ironic. Dark shapes are suddenly visible, and Octavia struggles to remain unheard as she works to draw near. She can't allow herself to be detected. As Octavia gets close she thinks she is able to make out female figures, naked under the night sky, and that wasn't disconcerting. Most of the women on this world paraded half dressed, even Semiramis when she had been covered in all her feathers, and finest leathers was still half naked. Yet as Octavia manages to draw near to these others she realizes unlike the locals, with their blue, azure, and sapphire skin tones, the aliens she now has come upon are black like the night sky they are under, nay, darker even.

The need for subterfuge diminished. The aliens so dark of skin begin to make a racket. They are howling, shrieking and soon screaming their heads off, as if they want to rattle the nerves of every living thing in a massive radius. After a few moments of the screaming, what Octavia now must consider to be their war cry, they begin to advance. They are moving on the *Dine'e* village, and toward the central longhouse of the village. Indeed, they move to surround it. There is a commotion coming from the longhouse, and Octavia takes it to be the sound of people fleeing in near panic. It sounds like the foot traffic is hurried, yet it doesn't seem as if anyone is being trampled in a mad rush. People are in flight, yet there isn't a stampede, not yet.

The aliens move in, around, and then beyond the *Dine'e* Village Longhouse, and Octavia follows with care. When she gets to the doors on the near side of the long house she comes upon a sight that chills her to the bone. While the leading men of *Aborto Espontáneo Blanco* are not going to get their hands on Semiramis, it looks like the aliens already have her, and they are no way shy about rough handling. While Morganti is safe, or so it seems, surrounded by the Soldier Girls as she is, Semiramis is the whole reason Morganti is here. Without Semiramis there is no deal for mineral rights. Octavia knows she must act, to standstill doing nothing is failure. Then Octavia sees how the aliens stand, a circle, a too perfect circle, and the way they hold their spears. The aliens are standing in a concentric circle surrounding Morganti and the Soldier Girls as the aliens each carry a highly metallic lance. Each lance begins to glow, and Octavia realizes what's happening and she screams a loud "No!" as she begins to dash toward Morganti and the Soldier Girls.

Octavia never reaches her people. She never even reaches the circle. She could have cut down, knifed or clubbed anyone of those aliens in an effort to protect Morganti, the Soldier Girls, or even Semiramis. Except there was a blur as everything went out of focus, then there was a flash as if everything turned really bright with white light, and then Octavia was someplace else. She was crouched and still. Even though she had been running, now for some unknown reason she wasn't. Octavia looks about and sees all the bright light is coming from the platform she's now finds herself upon. A quick look about and her eyes find the Chief and Captain Jack, both of them at a console. "What did you do?" she roars with rage.

"I hid your transition in theirs. It was the best way to get you out and remain undetected," Captain Jack tells her.

"What are you talking about?" demands a still very angry Octavia. She looks around more, seeing the other members of the deck crew from the *Dowager's Daughter*, and about three of those boys in the cream colored silk pajamas, the ones who work for Morganti.

"Don't yell at me, Octavia! I'm working under pressure, and we have to keep our heads!" Captain Jack shouts back.

"Wait, where are we?" asks Octavia.

"Welcome to the *Dowager's Dagger*," Captain Jack tells her with a wave of her arms.

"You said transition? Only Arcadians are capable of doing that, Jack," Octavia says.

"We are now on a ship that has limited transition capabilities. Also it seems this ship has cloaking ability and stealth shielding that make it virtually invisible," Responds the Captain.

"I need to know what happened. I need to know where everyone went," says Octavia.

"I'm pretty sure they are on the *Iowa*," Captain Jack tells her.

Octavia stands there, staring at Jack, no idea what to say next.

"Look, the crew and I have been looking this thing over, and we think we can maneuver this ship pretty close to the Arcadian Flagship, especially considering how distracted they must be," Captain Jack tells her.

"How distracted?" Octavia asks.

"They just did a major transition operation. Even if they re-discovered and to some extent mastered the technology it is still pretty difficult thing do. Any transition operation is a risky proposal," Captain Jack says.

"The transition operation is done now and thank you for risking my butt, Captain," Octavia replies.

"It is always safer with one person, and the fact that I had their array as a piggy back, to use for focus, made it all the easier," Captain Jack tells her.

"You mean those spears really were a transition array?" Octavia asks. "I mean that's what I thought, I just couldn't be sure."

"They were, and now we need to work on a plan to get our people back," says Captain Jack.

"How close can you get us? And come on Jack, you are talking about an Arcadian Fleet Battleship. How many other Arcadian assets are in the area? You better have a great plan as well as a level of stealth and cloak that even the best Arcadian sensors can't see through. No one has that Jack, no one has better toys than the Arcadians," says Octavia.

"Belazar has been able to get the better of Arcadia when it comes to stealth and cloak numerous times. The Arcadians tend to overlook stealth and cloaked maneuvers because they have so much overwhelming force at their disposal. Did you know they can make batteries that seem to have a near infinite life span? Anyway, I'm still looking at what this new ship can do. I think I can sneak right up on that fat flagship of theirs, and while we hide under their belly, we can work out a plan to get our people back," Captain Jack says.

****

We find ourselves in the middle of a circular chamber and still surrounded by what Semiramis calls the *Destroyers* or *Annareta*. What idiot thought up a name like that, I don't know. Yet that's what we hear her call them at one point.

"Don't try to fight the Annareta, or they will kill you, with glee," Semiramis tells us.

The monsters are all looking at us like they can't wait for their next chance at a kill. If they weren't something like twice my size I wouldn't be so intimidated. Also if they didn't have like six arms, claws and fangs... that's also intimidating. Maybe it would be different if we still had our guns. Only problem with that is we had been sitting for evening meal, and then we were at community story time hearing everything Semiramis had to say about her salad days. The long guns had been set aside some place safe. I had been lax about security, and now my employer and her *'client'* were paying for it. Although from what Semiramis says, and what I can see, whatever force we Soldier Girls could bring to bear would only put us on the losing end. The Annareta really do look that fierce, and they outnumber us three to one. The curious thing is that the Annareta are nothing like the fabled Arcadians most of creation talks about, yet so few have ever seen. *'I heard from my cousin who knows a guy who says he saw an Arcadian once, big as life, for like a whole half second before he went around a corner,'* and that is the kind of thing you hear, never much more.

While we stand here, four Soldier Girls and the two Luminaries we are supposed to be protecting, a man suddenly enters the chamber, a rather human looking man, and he surveys the situation. Shortly he begins to billow orders as if in a panic.

"God Good, you idiots! Some of them still have side arms in plain sight! You haven't even been about disarming them! So you haven't even searched them, I am sure of it, because you have been just standing around!" the man shouts. He looks to be an officer of high rank. "Once of your ploys to provoke them into attacking you, I know it!" he then goes on.

"Watch your mouth, Brackenbok!" shouts one of the monsters, the one wearing the silver belly chain.

"You've been too busy gloating, Alcina! That's why the prisoners are not secured. Disarm them! Search them! Get them into bonds! The Princess would see them, and I wish to interrogate them! So please just do your job!" the officer called Brackenbok commands, and I note that he's shouting at the only one to wear the silver belly chain. It seems strange. The monsters don't regard him as if he is in charge, or has any rank they need acknowledge at all. That is at odds with the impression I got from the man. He seems entirely to be a senior officer; I mean he has all the airs of such a man. Then the officer called Brackenbok, done billowing his commands, he leaves.

Alcina, that's what Brackenbok called her, she makes a gesture, and suddenly the monsters move to take what weapons we were left with, they search us, and then bind our wrists. One thing of note about the search: those girls certainly showed they have slow hands.

Well, only we Soldier Girls are bound. Not Semiramis and Morganti, they are pushed off to the side as if a secondary consideration. After we are cuffed behind our backs we are then made to kneel, all in a row. It's not the worst humiliation I've ever faced.

Long minutes go by before anything else happens; every moment is uncomfortable, and very tense. Recall we are surrounded by devil-girls, each and every one with a spear that she appears all too eager to use. Then the Princess arrives. The guy who seems like a senior officer is following her, yet she looks to be trying to give him the brush off as she comes. Perhaps she also found him to be mouthy. Perhaps he's just a tiresome fellow?

"If my so-called sister and her supposed sisters are in there with the prisoners then I am sure whatever danger I could face is minimal!" she is saying in what I take to be her *light* tone of command. Of course what I see when she comes fully into view is something so confusing I have no idea what to make of it.

"Oh my God, look, a school girl with three eyeballs," Tiger says good and loud, talking about what we must take to be the Arcadian Princess, and of course Tiger's every word rings with laughter. For that matter, *why is the Princess dressed like a school girl?* The all black sailor's jumper top looks good on her, she wears it well, yet I have to wonder why she even has it on?

"She's like one of those reverse albinos or something," Tiger goes on.

"Will you shut the hell up?" I hiss at my sniper.

"Will everyone please watch their language, the blasphemy is never appropriate!" Green says, hissing in me much the same way I hissed at Tiger.

The Princess, I can't tell if she stares at us like we are rubbish or just something weirder than she has ever seen before. She is a Princess, so God only knows how cloistered a life she's led. White is just on my left and she chooses now to start jabbering questions into my ear.

"She isn't blue. I thought all Arcadians were blue? She looks to be leucistic, how can she be leucistic and be one of their royals? I don't understand," the girl is yapping at me with no pause to hear an answer, *as if I have one*. I'm too worried about how this Princess is looking at us. A look like that usually means trouble. I really have a bad feeling about this, I mean it's like there is a buzzing in my head.

"Most Arcadians are blue," the Princess says to White, with a warm smile on her face. Then she's looking us over one after the other until the warm smile disappears. Yet she goes on talking about her people, *the Arcadians*. "Some are black, some are white, most are blue," she goes on in a casual voice. She walks by us all, every Soldier Girl that has been bound and made to kneel before her. My knees start to hurt. Then the Princess takes a few steps toward Semiramis and Morganti. She looks them over for a few moments, and then she goes to stand before us all. The Princess takes a stance with her feet shoulder length apart, and then places her hands behind her back, like parade rest. Then she begins a kind of address. Or she tries, because it seems as if she has some kind of headache. I understand, like I said there's some kind of buzzing going on inside my head. Anyway, the Princess gets herself together enough to speak: "I am Armida. This Arcadian Task Force has been sent here to quell any chaos affecting this system, and to show our flag. A recent engagement didn't go our way, and we must investigate the probability of a spy in our navy that was revealed here, in this very star system. So, do any of you have anything you want to say?"

"My head hurts," Tiger shares with the room.

Armida gives her a funny and very long look. Ultimately a really strained expression comes over her face.

"Really, it's like some kind of hornets next has been poked," Tiger says.

"Be quiet, it's something to do with this room, everyone has a buzzing in their heads. Must be the electrical conduits," Green tells her, trying to shush Tiger. Except she is wrong, I think.

"This is a secure conference room. Isolated, and with shielding from electromagnetic fields. The problem is not the conduits," says Armida, and the way she is looking at all of us Soldier Girls, it's making me so nervous, and that's in addition to the fact I'm being held captive. Also, I'm seeing some disconcerting things in my peripheral vision. The Annareta seem to have sudden headaches as well. The one addressed as *Alcina*, she seems to have the same kind of look on her face as does the Princess. Why are we the ones being stared at? It's the giant black girls who are walking around naked. God, why won't my head stop buzzing? We see Armida shake her head, trying to clear out the infernal buzzing, and she walks over toward Semiramis and Morganti. If this were any other sort of situation the frightened looks on their faces would be so amusing. Except this is awful, I mean I feel really awful. I hate being a prisoner, especially in front of the boss of my boss. God, I wish the Major was here to affect some kind of rescue. When the weird Princess Armida is a conversational distance from Semiramis and Morganti she begins to talk with them. "You are a local dignitary, aren't you?" she asks Semiramis.

"I am the Queen," Semiramis replies, showing that side of her we are most familiar. I mean suddenly she is filled with condescension broadcasting inward sense of superiority to all others.

"And you are the intrusive business woman?" Armida asks Morganti.

"A woman has to be aggressive, or she won't be in business," Morganti replies.

"Without question," Armida says in response, and though from where I am I can't see her face, I feel like she is speaking with a visible light in her eyes. Then her stance changes and she turns her gaze back our way, back to the Soldier Girls. Armida, while waving her finger at us, she looks at the chief monster, the one the officer called *Alcina*, and Armida begins shouting: "They are knockoffs! The buzzing! Its data relay! Wireless data routers inside all of us have been activated because these four haven't been connected to a network for God only knows how long!"

I have no idea what she is talking about, and every one of my Soldier Girls is looking from one to the other for explanation.

Alcina raises her great silver lance and begins to walk my way.

"I didn't say kill anyone! Why is that always your answer to everything?" Armida shouts.

"A dead enemy can't hurt us," Alcina replies, and the cold in her voice makes me think of a chilled abattoir.

"They can't hurt us! Look at the data packs they are transmitting, the code! These four automatons are clearly purloined and reverse engineered technology!" Armida is saying, looking at us with so much excitement.

"Hey! Watch your mouth!" Tiger shouts, drawing a harsh look from both Armida and Alcina. Really, calling us *automatons* is tantamount to frat boys talking about the interchangeability of girls from the freshman class. Or something worse, like a racial epithet.

"We aren't automatons! Morganti took the chips out!" White cries out, sounding so much like a child.

"Shush, dear," I tell her.

"Yet now we know you are," Green comments, her tone low while her eyes bore in on Armida.

"What say you?" asks Armida, her eyes, and those of her *sister* Alcina locked on Green.

"We don't listen for signals, yet we do look at the way people walk, or we used to, and the way you walk, Princess, you and these Annareta are machine people, aren't you?" Green responds. When no one says anything, Green goes on: "We once were at a camp when a genetically engineered girl and her robot came walking through. While we knew the robot for what she was, we knew the girl was engineered. We could tell by the swing of her hips. It was all in her gate and stride. Hips don't lie, and no one born of woman walks the way that girl did."

Making the moment odder and more uncomfortable than it already is, Morganti has dashed over, leaving Semiramis, and coming around to stand before us. She's giving Green such a hard stare.

"Yeah, hard to believe I'm the only one who put it all together, and it took this long, but we've met your daughter, your genetically engineered daughter. Same hair, same face, eyes, so much of you in her, yet she's twice your height and ten times as strong as any man, at the least, so now we know the Widow of Market Town used to be a genetic engineer?" says Green. I want to punch her in the face. We are getting fired, so fired. I've never had to look for a new job before and it scares me.

"Just shut up," Morganti is hissing at Green.

"Just shut up all of you!" Armida shouts. Then she is looking at Morganti, and she asks: "So you want to be the mining magnate of *Aborto Espontáneo Blanco*? Why should the Arcadian Empire go through you when we could just set up our own operation?"

"The people here prefer to call their world *Lupus Formosus*, and I've already made the deal with Queen Semiramis. I don't think she has any inclination to go back on her word, now with me," Morganti replies.

They both look to Semiramis for a moment, and she gives a little nod.

"You will need a shipping agent, a distribution network. And I am sure you will want a buyer who can pay top of the market," Armida says, and again we see that gleam in her eye and the smile of her lips.

"I'll have to consult with my partner," Morganti says, her eyes shifting toward Semiramis.

I swear in that moment the one wearing the belly chain, Alcina, she has a 'kill them all' look on her face. So we know why she doesn't conduct the family business. How is it mechanicals like Armida and Alcina are sisters, and Armida is the *'Princess'* of the biggest galactic super empire there ever was? How did the Arcadians become such an empire with such little known about them? I've got some catching up to do. Anyway, not much else matters because Morganti and Armida are smiling at each other, a sure sign the deal is done, and Semiramis is not frowning, or looking at anyone in murderous rage, so she must be happy. Yet Semiramis lets us know what thoughts are on her mind.

"Seventy Percent will be my people's share of your gross profit," Semiramis announces to the room.

Suddenly Morganti and Armida are taken by surprise.

"Seven percent will be a more appropriate number," Morganti offers as her counter proposal.

"No, my people must have at least double that, at least twice as much as seven, so seventy is the number," Semiramis replies.

"You will settle for twice seven percent?" asks Morganti.

"It must be at least twice seven, as I know your numbers, so seventy," Semiramis insists.

"At least twice seven, so I could offer you fourteen?" Morganti says.

"Perhaps that will due," Semiramis says, looking suspicious at the other woman.

"Fourteen?" Morganti offers.

"And the little rebellion you were facing will be quelled by the assistance of the Arcadians? Perhaps even the Annareta?" adds Armida.

"Agreed," Alcina says, sounding very eager. The girl must like a scrap.

Semiramis, perhaps she fancies the idea of returning home with a contingent of killing machines at her side, and she nods. The whole room can see the fire in her eyes. There will be blood when the Queen comes home.

Armida then turns to us Soldier Girls, asking: "By the way, do any of you know anything about a spy in my navy?"

That's the whole place shakes with an explosion.

✳✳✳✳

The *Red Unicorn* and the rest of her battle group came out of their space jump employing an extant rift in normal space. When the natural breach was forced to a much wider aperture it left a bloody red wound in the fabric of reality. With the *Red Unicorn* leading the formation it was as if a mist of blood trailed the old super dreadnought class warship. Her sisters, the black and silver unicorns, they fly through this seeming mist of blood following their flagship.

"Admiral Mallakastra, we are clear of the space rift, and within particle weapons range of the Arcadian ship *Iowa*. Within sixty seconds we will have a targeting solution for missiles and ballistic weapons," the operations officer reports.

"What are the Arcadians doing? Have they detected us?" asks the Admiral.

"They are dispersed, a loose formation at best, and they do not appear to have detected us, Admiral. There appears to be no reaction yet," the operations officer responds.

"They are in orbit about the planet?" asks Admiral Mallakastra.

"Yes, Admiral," reports the operations officer.

"Our window for attack before detection, or before they move into the shadow of the planet?" asks Admiral Mallakastra.

"Only moments remain, my Admiral," reports the weapons officer.

"Every weapons system that reports a target lock, to avenge my brother's humiliation, fire!" commands the Admiral, her voice a cutting screech.

The orders of Mallakastra were relayed to the other ships. Only a moment after the *Red Unicorn* discharged her particle cannons, and then launched her ballistics, her sister ships were doing the same. Everyone targeted the Arcadian battle ship *Iowa*, and as soon as the first salvo was complete the weapons crews of the Bellazar fleet were preparing to fire again.

For us onboard the Arcadian ship things felt scary. We were on board one of the most powerful warships in all creation. Add to that the *Iowa* is part of a squadron of similar warships. We all know there was only one power in the galaxy that has the power and will to challenge the Arcadians like this, so they must be near. Indeed, they attack now. They are close enough to shoot, yet far enough to not yet be detected somehow even with their every weapon popping off.

The deck shakes and I worry we may be tossed. The Princess looks like she is about to say something important when there is a queer flash of light. Not bright, yet a definite flash, and then we all see Major Octavia standing before us. I see her toss a series of devices about the compartment with a single flourish even as she appears, and then she tosses another device to be caught by Morganti. I hear Alcina scream with bloodlust and battle fury as she leaps at the Major. There is another flash, and then we are someplace else, in another compartment.

We are still bound, still on our knees, the Major standing over us, and Morganti nearby.

"Did you left Semiramis behind?" Morganti asks the Major, letting everyone know she still has her priorities.

"No she's right there, how we might get her a ride home, I haven't thought about," the Major says as she kneels to set me free. Most of us look, and Semiramis is standing there just as she was, except we are somewhere other than where we were.

"They took our guns, all our gear," White says, with some distress in her voice.

"It's just gear. We can replace everything," the Major says to the girl as she begins to turn loose her bonds, and I swear I've never heard the Major sound so kind.

Then I feel the ship moving under us just a split second before I hear the Chief shout: "Captain is initiating hard maneuvers, brace yourselves!" Then the man is walking straight up to me, and he tries to guide me to a hand rail. I give him a look meant to warn him off. He gives me a smile and my jaw drops. I have no idea how to respond. What is wrong with this grinning idiot? He turns away attending other things, and then someone else is beside me. Actually behind me, and it's Green.

"You are so lucky, and I am becoming jealous," Green says to me.

"What are you on about?" I ask, my face surely twisted by confusion.

"White has her rich man, Tiger has her hunter, and you have your sailor. What have I got? No one," Green says.

"White has a nutty fat man obsessed with her, Tiger has the fat man's poorly behaved cousin doing nothing more than taking her for long walks, and I have to put up with some middle aged merchant marine's infatuation. What have you got to be jealous about?" I demand, trying to keep my voice down.

"White is in love with a man who is in love with her. Tiger could possibly fall in love, or just go on another pleasant walk. And you have a decent fellow interested in you, a working class man who shows more deference to you than he does anyone else. You could do so much worse," Green explains.

I'm about to tell her to shut her fly trap, then I hear Morganti get on an intercom asking: "What are you doing, dear Jack?"

"I was about to do a blind space jump, and then I remembered we have a space station here?" Captain Jack says over the intercom.

"Is the *Void Helkein* under attack?" the Major asks.

"Not yet, but seven ships are out there starting the biggest brawl I ever did see," Captain Jack replies.

"Tell the *Void Helkein* we are on our way, and they need to move away from the battle site," Morganti tells him.

"Will do," Captain Jack replies. "Umm, you do know that means the *Void Helkein* will be moving very close to the planetary nadir?" he asks. Was that fear we just heard in the voice of Captain Jack?

"I'm sure it won't prove to be that much of an issue," Morganti replies.

"Moving to Black Knight orbit then," responds the Captain.

We follow the *Void Helkein* to station keeping proximate to the southern pole of *Lupus Formosus*, and then we sit there watching the outer space slugfest. Networking the sensor array of both the *Void Helkein* and the *Dowager's Dagger* we have a pretty good view of the fight, and it is a vivid spectacle. The Arcadians have more ships, yet they seem to be outweighed over all. We quickly see how they are suited to fight above their weight class. While the Bellazar ships are massive monsters, the Arcadians are sleek, nimble, and make their blows count. They are dancing fighters. You would think ships like theirs fight by the *death of a thousand needles* strategy, yet what looks like little blows actually turn out to be rather deep cuts, and scary injuries for the enemy. The Arcadian ship *Iowa* suffers badly for having been the first hit, the first to suffer sever wounds, and a part of me worries for Armida. Why I would worry about a princess I've only met once, and while I was a prisoner, I don't know. Maybe I liked her, she seemed fair, tough but fair. If you can't respect that in a person, you got problems. From where we sat we saw the action of the void battle play out, and it was a good show for all.

A bit of crafty strategy was the moment when Morganti and Major Octavia pushed Semiramis forward so she could see the battle on every screen, in all its dramatic glory. In the course of her life the woman had endured long hunts, stretches of time in the wilderness I found impressive, and I used to do long range reconnaissance patrols. Her first time in space and she gets to observe the massive battleships of the massive stellar empires slugging it out. My first time in space I was in cold storage, and locked up awaiting a court martial where I was presented as actual evidence against myself. Semiramis stands there, still barely dressed save a few pieces of animal hide, and clearly she is awed. I don't think any of her people have ever been off planet before now. The woman began to shake in her limbs as she tried to take in the immensity of it all. This is when Morganti took Semiramis from the cockpit of the *Dowager's Dagger* to the *Void Helkein*, and I assume to be pampered by those pajama boys Morganti had attending her. I'm no deal maker, yet I will suppose that this is when Morganti truly sealed the deal. She had Semiramis alone, in an environment entirely unfamiliar. Either Semiramis was going to go berserk, or she was going to entirely fold.

The battle was still going on, and while we wanted to know the conclusion, we were knackered. Everyone was hungry, tired, and our nerves were shot. Well, tired, not so hungry. Then that pest the Chief of the Boat, he walks up to me with a big cup and straw. With the silly grin on his face he says: "I brought you a milkshake."

I try to show him by my face how apprehensive I am about... Well I'm not sure. I took the cup without thinking about it, and with some hesitation I put the straw to my lips. Then I realize my Soldier Girls have dismissed themselves without my word, and I'm about to say something.

Then Green turns about, saying: "Sack time, if someone needs us, they will come for us." Then she winks at me with a grin that seems positively wicked, and I have no idea what that's all about.

"Where are they going? We haven't been assigned billets here," I say. Then I notice the Chief is still looking at me, still smiling, and I ask: "What has you in so much cheer?"

"The girl I like came home safe, and she let me buy her a milkshake. Considering how my social life usually goes, this is a banner event for me," he replies.

"You are an odd duck," I tell him, and sip more of the milkshake.

"They can find their own billets, they're big girls. And you, Commander, you have earned a break," the Chief tells me.

"As if you would know," I say, looking at him.

"I got three of my own, if you may recall," the Chief says.

The Major reappears, and she says to me: "You already got all the other girls down for a rest?

Good work, Commander. You and the Chief should go relax while you can."

Then she is walking past me to the cockpit of our new ship, and once she is a pace or two from where Captain Jack sits minding the helm, she turns backward, and makes a gesture as if sending us away. It's as if she's making me spend time alone with the Chief. I'll never forgive her. Yet I will drink more of his milkshake.

Epilogue

A lot of things happened in the following weeks.

We went on vacation. Business was conducted. It was a kind of working vacation. That's the best we can hope for these days, and I can promise you it is still better than the life we had before the Major and the Widow.

Semiramis was accompanied by Alcina and the Annareta to reclaim her throne. She went back home and then followed a brief period of madness that left a lot of people dead. Semiramis settled scores, and the Annareta were more than happy to aid their new political ally in such work. It is like Semiramis and Alcina found something they could do together. I know, it's creepy to think about.

Irwin Grossman arrived and his time was split several ways. He stepped in to help Morganti work out the rough edges of her agreement with the Arcadians, and he negotiated with the Bellazar authorities to relinquish any previous claim they had to *Lupus Formosus*. Basically he paid them off. The man puzzles me because when I see him with White, when he isn't attending business or finance, he's jelly. Before my girl White, Irwin Grossman, the big business juggernaut of the galaxy, is a bowl of giggling jelly. I swear, when the two of them are alone, or they have at least forgotten anyone else is present, they become like a pair of kittens, or love bugs on laughing gas. They are the couple other couples hate to compare their relationship to, and I know because I was scammed into a double date with them. I had to sit at a small table for a gourmet meal with the two of them and the Chief. Jason, his name is Jason, and if we are dating, and I'm not saying we are, then I should call him by name. That was a good meal, I just wonder if *gourmet* really means *ultra-small portions*?

Irwin had brought his shaggy cousin with him, and he was gone just as suddenly taking Tiger with him. They had their rifles, their knapsacks full of dry rations and other bushwhacking gear, and I must suppose they were happy.

Green and I felt the need to see for ourselves how the *Void Helkein* was operating since that moment when we were briefly plugged in to operate as the conjoined controlling mind of the monstrous thing. We found the Janus Control system occupied by new *control nodes*. That's what they called them. The technicians had these two anemic looking girls in the couches, all plugged in and running the whole show with only the slightest oversight. They were creepy little things, I can assure you, yet they seemed to be doing the job.

Businesses commenced, and as business is want to do business showed sign it would expand. Tiger came back with the shaggy cousin after about two weeks, a period they both seemed to spend avoiding soap and water, and the shaggy cousin, Seiko is his name, he began to tell Irwin about all the potential the planet had to offer for charter hunting trips and wilderness retreats. I'm glad I don't have to sit through that meeting with Semiramis. I suppose she will demand eighty percent of the profits, and then agree to the much higher number of sixteen, as she knows our numbers.

Author's Note

It has taken me a very long time to complete this novel, yet I am sure this is not the last story if Octavia Pomona & The Soldier Girls I am going to tell. Only time can say. I suffered the death of my mother while writing this novel and the loss was terrible. The grief I have suffered temporarily left me unable to write, and wondering if I would ever do so again. Losing my mother has been so hard on me that even as I put these words on the page I am still picking up pieces.

If you are reading this, I want to thank you from the bottom of my heart. My readers are my best friends and I will love you forever.

Made in United States
Orlando, FL
30 September 2024